The Author

MORDECAI RICHLER was born in Montreal, Quebec, in 1931. Raised there in the working-class Jewish neighbourhood around St. Urbain Street, he attended Sir George Williams College (now a part of Concordia University). In 1951 he left Canada for Europe, settling in London, England, in 1954. Eighteen years later, he moved back to Montreal.

Novelist and journalist, screenwriter and editor, Richler, one of the most acclaimed contemporary writers, has spent much of his career chronicling, celebrating, and criticizing the Montreal and the Canada of his youth. Whether the settings of his fiction are St. Urbain Street or European capitals, his major characters never forsake the Montreal world that shaped them. His most frequent voice is that of the satirist, rendering an honest account of his times with care and humour.

Richler's many honours include two Governor General's Awards and unnumerable other awards for fiction, journalism, and screenwriting.

Mordecai Richler resides in Montreal.

THE NEW CANADIAN LIBRARY

Mordecai Richler

COCKSURE

With an Afterword by Margaret Drabble

The following dedication appeared in the original edition:

FOR JACK AND HAYA

First published in Canada in 1968 by McClelland & Stewart
This New Canadian Library edition 1996

Canadian Cataloguing in Publication Data

Richler, Mordecai, 1931–
Cocksure

(New Canadian library)
ISBN 0-7710-3458-X

I. Title II. Series.

PS8535.I38C6 1996 C813'.54 C95-932639-1
PR9199.3.R53C6 1996

The publishers acknowledge the support of the Canada Council and the Ontario Arts Council for their publishing program.

The lines quoted on pages 104-105 are from *The Adventurers* by Harold Robbins, copyright © 1966 by Harold Robbins, reprinted by permission of Trident Press.

Typesetting by M&S, Toronto
Cover layout by Andrew Skuja

Printed and bound in Canada by Webcom Limited

McClelland & Stewart Inc.
The Canadian Publishers
481 University Avenue
Toronto, Ontario
M5G 2E9

1 2 3 4 5 00 99 98 97 96

Cocksure

One

DINO TOMASSO BRAKED before the high, familiar gates with the coupling snakes woven into the wrought iron. It was not necessary for him to show a pass, but he had to wait, drumming his three-fingered left hand against the steering wheel, while the armed, black-uniformed guard threw the lever that opened the gates and waved Tomasso's AC Cobra 427 through. Tomasso turned into the winding, cypress-lined driveway, whistling happily until he spotted Laughton sitting by the poolside.

Laughton, one of several doctors attached to the Star Maker's medical unit, was drinking with Gail, a pretty nurse in a bikini. "Time for a quick snort?" he asked.

"No. Sorry," Tomasso said, his voice wobbly.

"How you keeping?"

"Lousy. *Honestly.*"

"Hold on a minute." With a wink for Gail, Laughton whipped out an eye chart from under his towel and pointed a swizzle stick at the fifth line: U F J Z B H Q A. "Let's go," he said.

Tomasso reached for a tissue and wiped his forehead and the back of his thick, pleated neck. He squinted. "I'll try my best. J," he said, "T Y Z B . . . um . . . S . . . N . . . How am I doing?"

"You're faking, you bastard."

"You mean," Tomasso said, radiating innocence, "I may need glasses?"

Gail shrieked with laughter.

"You're a card, Dino," Laughton said, "you really are."

Tomasso laughed too, but ingratiatingly, without smiling. "How's tricks?" he asked.

Laughton indicated the blinking red light and locked doors of the mobile operating theater. The Star Maker's defrocked priest stood alongside, commiserating with one of the spare-parts men.

"Oh, no," Tomasso said.

"Don't jump to conclusions. It's all because of the new nurse."

"Miss McInnes?"

"Bitch hadn't been told about the deep-freeze."

"*She defrosted*," Gail squealed.

"Holy shit!"

With trembling hand, Tomasso flicked the AC Cobra 427 into gear and sped toward the big house, pursued by their laughter. My God, my God, he thought, sliding out of the car, favoring his right leg, which was artificial.

The ageless, undying Star Maker reclined in his customary wheelchair. Behind, sending a shiver through Tomasso yet again, there loomed the familiar portrait of the pernicious Chevalier d'Éon, at once the Star Maker's hero and heroine.

"Do you know why I sent for you, Dino?"

When Tomasso was summoned from Hollywood to the Star Maker's mansion in Las Vegas, he calculated, not unreasonably, that he was at last to be designated crown prince of the empire. After all these years of sacrifice, he thought, unstinting labor and operations, he would be officially recognized heir apparent.

"No," Tomasso lied hopefully.

"We hope to acquire a publishing house and a film studio

in England. I want you to go to London and look after my interests there."

Oh, no, this wasn't making him crown prince. This was even worse than a demotion. It was banishment.

Tomasso, who had been raised in the motion picture business, knew that London was not where you sent an heir apparent to be tested – it was the place whereto you shipped schlemiels to make son-in-law movies.

Son-in-law movies were produced by a studio chief's cousins, uncles, and sons-in-law, who had to be given something more than their fingers to twiddle: otherwise it wouldn't look nice for the family. Once, Tomasso remembered, these retarded relations were put in charge of the popcorn concession or distribution to ozoners, but that became too big; then they were allowed to sell rerun rights to TV, but then that became too big too; and so finally they were sent to England with blessings. A new breed of remittance men. In London, making zero pictures with zero actors, they still cost the family money, but the losses were negligible.

"I'm not going," Tomasso said defiantly.

"In twenty-five years, Dino, you have never said no to me before."

Tomasso looked at the floor, steadying himself.

"I have no heir. You are my son, Dino."

How many times had he heard that before? Raising his head, astonished at his own courage, Tomasso said, "Go fuck yourself."

Slowly, slowly, the Star Maker raised hands to face, shielding the bad eye. In the pause that ensued Tomasso dug his fingernails into the palms of his hands, making them bleed.

"Go . . . Why, you're committing suicide, Dino."

Tomasso fell to his knees. "Forgive me, Star Maker."

The Star Maker's face creased. It was, Tomasso supposed, a smile. "But why, Dino?"

"Oh, Star Maker, please, it's just that I dared to dream of

bigger things when you sent for me. The words leaped out. I didn't mean it."

The Star Maker pressed a button, summoning his private secretary, Miss Mott. The Star Maker pressed another button and they were joined by two black-uniformed motorcycle riders.

"Say it again, Dino."

"I'd cut my tongue out first, Star Maker."

"No, no. Miss Mott, get this down. I'll want eight copies, witnessed and signed by Mr. Tomasso."

"But it was a slip of the tongue, so help me. We don't need witnesses."

"It's for your own protection, Dino."

"Is it?"

"You said it to me first."

"I've given you the best years of my life, Star Maker. Anything you asked, I did."

"We'll take it from the top. I said, quote, I want you to go to London and look after my interests there, unquote. You said, quote, I'm not going, unquote. I said, quote, I have no heir. You are my son, Dino, unquote. Then you said, quote . . . ?"

"I said . . . I said . . . Maybe you heard me wrong, Star Maker?"

"Come on, Dino. *Then you said, quote?*"

Trembling, Tomasso repeated what he had said.

"Can you beat that?" the Star Maker asked, actually laughing.

Miss Mott's eyes widened.

"I'm unwell," Tomasso said, sobbing. "I was possessed."

"To think that you've been with me all these years and I never suspected your true –"

Tomasso seized the smaller of the Star Maker's hands and kissed it.

"Tell me, Dino, have you ever thought this before?"

"Never!"

"Keeping it to yourself all these years?"

"No!"

There was another pause, before the Star Maker chuckled and asked, "Say it once more, Dino."

"I couldn't."

"Just once."

The black-uniformed riders stepped closer to Tomasso. So he obliged, but in the smallest possible voice.

"It's amazing," the Star Maker said. "Coming from you. How I've underestimated you all these years. . . ."

"What happens to me now, Star Maker?"

But the Star Maker seemed to be lost in a reverie. "Amazing."

"What happens to me?"

"To you? Why, I want you to go to London, as I said. If, after six months there, you feel the same way about England, you can come back and pick up any job you want here."

"You mean," Tomasso said incredulously, "you're giving me a second chance?"

"As long as I have no heir, you are my son, Dino. Will you go?"

"Will I go? Oh, Star Maker."

"Take this file with you, then. Study it."

"Oh, thank you," Tomasso said, fleeing.

The younger of the two black-uniformed riders unstrapped his gun. "I'll see to it," he said.

"No," the other rider protested, "it's my turn."

"Neither of you," the Star Maker said, "will do any harm to Dino."

"*After what he said to you?*"

"Because of what he said to me. Now beat it."

Tomasso, slumped behind the wheel of his Cobra 427, lit one cigarette off another, waiting for his heart to quiet. It was simply unknown for the Star Maker to give anyone a second chance, to forgive; therefore it must be true – the Star Maker, Blessed Be His Name, has not been mocking me all these years: I am like a son to him.

Whistling happily once more, Tomasso wheeled off the driveway, taking the left fork, a road which led to the villas by the lake where the favored stars were kept. He swept past the low-lying, windowless laboratory, turning left again when he came to the end of the humming fence; and, three miles down the road, he pulled in opposite the most elegant villa. The villa where Star Maker Productions' most valuable property, its greatest, all-time favorite box-office Star, lived.

Might as well look in and say hello, Tomasso thought, as the Star's next picture, a multimillion-dollar production, was to be made in England. *In England.* Maybe things are changing, Tomasso thought, his spirits rising still higher. Maybe a British production doesn't have to be small beans any more.

"Hi," Tomasso said, waving at the guard on duty. "Where's the big fella?"

"Resting," he said, puffing on his pipe.

"Still?"

"Yeah."

Tomasso stopped short when he came upon two used starlets lying on the living-room rug. They were nude. "God damn it," he said, turning indignantly on the guard, "how long have you been with us?"

"All of thirty years."

"Remember Goy-Boy II then, don't you?"

"Of course, sir."

"Then you certainly ought to know better. A pipe," he hissed, "in here? *Live ashes!*" And he yanked the pipe out of the guard's mouth, flinging it through the open window.

"Please don't report me, sir."

Tomasso, the contrite guard following after, entered the Star's bedroom without knocking and walked to the cupboard, where the Star was hanging. Tomasso pondered the

Star for a long time, poking, pinching, looking him up and down. Finally, satisfied, he shut the cupboard door softly. "He looks great."

"He is great."

"You said it. What's the script like?"

"Great."

"Great," Tomasso said. "Now you be careful, will you?" he added, stepping over the starlets.

"Yes, sir."

Not until he had boarded the Star Maker's Lear jet did Tomasso have time to consider the London file. The publishing firm the Star Maker was after was called Oriole; it was run by a lord. There were two senior editors, Hyman Rosen and Mortimer Griffin. Studying Griffin's photograph, at twenty thousand feet, Tomasso decided he was going to be trouble. He felt it in his bones.

Two

"YOUR TIME IS OVER," the big black African on the platform shouted, his smile lethal. "You're done for, you stupid white swine."

"That's the stuff," cried a man with a Welsh accent.

"You Anglo-Saxon pigs," the African said, still grinning. "You stupid British nits!"

Before Mortimer could intervene, Miss Ryerson was shaking her umbrella at the African. "Mr. Speaker," she began, with that in-built authority that had once been sufficient to make the fourth grade sit bolt upright, "we decent, God-fearing people of British origin want to support you –"

"Har," the African growled, flashing pearly teeth.

"– but when you stand up there, all cheekiness, it doesn't give us much encouragement, you know."

"Who in the hell wants you to support us, you stupid old woman!"

"Shoot," Agnes Laura Ryerson said to Mortimer.

"The English are an insult to humanity," the speaker continued. "The quicker they are liquidated the better."

A beet-faced gentleman, standing directly behind Mortimer and Miss Ryerson, touched his tweed cap, smiled, and said, "These black chaps are splendidly uninhibited, don't you think?"

Somebody flung a half-peeled banana at the speaker. Another man shouted, "Tell us if you're living here on National Assistance. *With your three black wives and eighteen kiddies.*"

Mortimer took Miss Ryerson firmly by the arm, leading her across Oxford Street and to the Corner House, stopping to collect the *Sunday Times* for them to study at tea. Unfortunately Miss Ryerson picked up the magazine section first, opening it at the glistening all-but-nude photograph of a sensual pop singer, a young man caressing a cat. The singer wished to star in a film about the life of Christ. Jesus, he was quoted as saying, was no square. But a real groovy cat.

Migod, Mortimer thought. Sweet, silver-haired Agnes Laura Ryerson was his fourth-grade teacher from Caribou, Ontario, and he had tried his utmost to discourage her from making this sentimental journey. Miss Ryerson's long-cherished fantasy picture of the mother country, more potent than any pot dream, was constructed almost entirely on literary foundations. Shakespeare, naturally, Jane Austen, *The Illustrated London News*, Kipling, Dickens, Beverly Baxter's London Letters in *Macleans*.

Together Miss Ryerson and Mortimer scanned the theater listings. As she made appreciative noises over her scones, he persuaded her that the Royal Shakespeare Company's latest venture into the theater of cruelty was not quite her cuppa. "It's vastly overrated," he insisted nervously.

Shoot. Miss Ryerson pursed her lips, displeased, inadvertently evoking for Mortimer the day she had given him five of the best on each hand for being caught with a copy of *Nana* in his desk. She simply had to go to the theater every night, she explained, for she had undertaken to write a weekly "Letter from London" for the *Presbyterian Church-Monitor of Southern Ontario*. "What do you know," she asked, "about this one?"

This one was a tender domestic comedy about a homosexual couple.

"Um, well, it's a bit naughty, I'm told."

They settled on a farce for Tuesday night. Monday, one of Mortimer's lecture nights, was out, unfortunately.

Oriole Press, where Mortimer was an editor, was still one of London's most distinguished publishing houses; that is to say, it had yet to be taken over and transmogrified by the Star Maker. Mortimer enjoyed his work and had reason to hope that he was being considered as the next editor-in-chief, the penultimate step toward a seat on the board of directors, his initials carved into the two-hundred-year-old round table. Oriole's celebrated oak. The saintly proprietor of Oriole Press, Lord Woodcock, had hinted at the appointment during a meeting with Mortimer at his Albany flat two years back. "Hodges," Lord Woodcock had said, referring to the then editor-in-chief, "is nearing the retirement age. It would be indelicate of me to say more, but I will tell you this much, Griffin; when the time comes I'll be damned if I'm going outside our family for a replacement." Which left Mortimer with one rival. Hy Rosen, his best friend.

Following in the footsteps of Lord Woodcock, a Fabian with the purest Christian motives, the younger editorial staff at Oriole Press was encouraged to make use of their leisure time by serving the larger community in one socially responsible form or another. Two nights weekly little Hy Rosen worked as a boxing instructor at a Stepney youth club. Mortimer chose to deliver a series of lectures on "Reading for Pleasure" at an evening college in Paddington, sponsored by one of England's more forward-looking trade unions. Mortimer's third lecture, on Monday night, dealt with Franz Kafka and naturally he made several allusions to the distinctively Jewish roots of his work. Afterwards, as he was gathering his notes together, a lachrymose little man approached him for the first time.

"I want to tell you, Professor Griffin, how much intellectual nourishment I got out of your lecture tonight."

"I'm glad you enjoyed it," Mortimer said, in a hurry to leave because he was supposed to meet Joyce at Hy and Diana Rosen's and it looked as if he was going to be late. But the lachrymose little man still stood resolutely before his desk.

His wisps of gray curly hair uncut and uncombed, he was a puny round-shouldered man with horn-rimmed spectacles, baleful black eyes, and a hanging lower lip. His shiny pinstriped gray suit was salted with dandruff around the shoulders. A hand-rolled cigarette drooped from his mouth, his eyes half shut against the smoke and ashes spilling unregarded to his jacket. "Why did you change your name?" he asked.

"I beg your pardon? Did you ask me why I changed my name?"

The man nodded.

"But I haven't. My name is Griffin. It always has been."

The man considered Mortimer with a sardonic, pitying smile. "You're a Jew," he said softly.

"You're mistaken."

The man chuckled.

"Really," Mortimer said. "What made you think –"

"All right. I'm mistaken. I made a mistake. Not to worry."

"Look here, if I were a Jew I wouldn't try to conceal it for a moment."

Still smiling, blinking his eyes, the man said, "There's no need to lose your temper, Professor *Griffin*. I made a mistake. If that's the way you want it."

"And I'm not a professor either. Mr. Griffin will do nicely."

"A man of your insights will be famous one day . . . like . . . like I. M. Sinclair. A scholar renowned wherever the intelligentsia meet. Thanks once more, *merci mille fois*, for tonight's intellectual feast. Good night, Mr. Griffin."

Good night.

Driving out to the Rosens' flat in Swiss Cottage, Mortimer smiled indulgently. Me Jewish, he thought, laughing out loud.

Joyce had eaten with the Rosens, and Diana, remembering how much Mortimer fancied chopped liver, had saved him an enormous helping. Seated in the living room, amid Hy's framed photographs of Abe (the Little Hebrew) Attell, Phil (Ring Gorilla) Bloom, Chrysanthemum Joe Choynski, Ruby (the Jewel of the Ghetto) Goldstein, Yussel the Mussel Jacobs, Benny Leonard, Barney Ross, and others, Mortimer told him about the lachrymose little man, concluding with ". . . and where in the hell he ever got the idea I was Jewish I'll never know."

Mortimer had anticipated laughter, a witty remark from Hy, perhaps. Instead there was silence. Nervy silence.

"Look, I don't mean I'd be ashamed –"

"Gee, thanks."

"– or that I was insulted that someone would think I was –"

"Ah ha."

"Christ, you know what I mean, Hy."

"You're goddamned right I do," Hy said, springing to his feet and removing his glasses.

Mortimer and Joyce left for home earlier than usual.

"Boy," Joyce said, "you certainly have a gift. Once you *have* put your foot into it you certainly know how to make matters worse."

"I thought they'd laugh. God, Hy's my best friend. He –"

"*Was*," Joyce said.

While Joyce was undressing in the bathroom, Mortimer slipped surreptitiously out of the bedroom, down the hall, and into Doug's room. Doug was just eight years old and having a peek at him as he slept gave Mortimer a wonderfully warm feeling inside. He had to watch it, though, because Joyce felt this was very *Saturday Evening Post* of him. Specially the kissing bit. She's right, too, Mortimer thought, as he gave Doug a hasty peck on the forehead and fled.

Joyce, Mortimer gathered, was still upset. "Come off it," he said. "You don't seriously think Hy thinks I'm an anti-Semite?"

Joyce raised one eyebrow slightly.

"Don't be ridiculous," he said. "Tomorrow the whole thing will be forgotten. Hy will make a joke of it."

Then they settled into bed with books. Back to back. Joyce, on her side, with *The Story of O*; Mortimer, on his side, with *The Best of Leacock*.

"They have an excellent sense of humor," Joyce said, "haven't they? There's Mort Sahl and Art Buchwald and –"

"Oh, for Christ's sake!"

"If I were you I'd phone him and apologize."

"There's no need. Damn it, I adore Hy. I've known him for years."

Three

"HE'S AT LEAST SEVEN inches taller than I am," Hy said. "I'd be giving him a good forty pounds and still he was too chicken-shit to put up his fists."

Hy bounced to his feet and pulled his shirt up high as his chin, revealing his narrow pigeon chest, his heart hammering, the ribs thrusting through.

"Punch me, luv. Let me have it."

"Oh, Hy, please," Diana said.

"No, no. Go ahead. All your might, now."

"But, Hy –"

"*I said punch me.*"

Diana pulled back obligingly, grimaced, and simulated a mighty blow to Hy's tense, flat stomach.

"Didn't feel a thing," Hy said, letting his shirt drop.

"But Mortimer didn't mean to offend you," Diana protested.

"One day in Holland, at a time when we were bloody short on ammo, the major called for a volunteer to lead a recon into the forest. I stepped forward immediately and you know what one of my *brother* officers said just loud enough for me to catch? 'They're all the same,' he said. 'Pushy.' But if I hadn't been the first to step forward he would have put me down for a coward. They're all the same, goys, what do I need 'em for?"

"What about me?" Diana asked, nuzzling him.

All at once Hy gathered Diana's long blond hair in his fist and yanked.

"Oh, Hy! Hy! Please let me go!"

"Come on," Hy said, pulling her. "Into the bedroom. Let's put that big goysy ass of yours to work."

Diana, who towered over Hy, contrived to be dragged, protesting, into the bedroom.

"Oh, I know you in this state," she said. "You're going to be too big for me. You're going to hurt me."

Hy's laugh was gargantuan, charged with menace.

"You filthy Jew," Diana hollered, turning round and stooping for Hy to unzip her. "You always have only one thing in mind."

"British twat," Hy said, butting her in the belly and diving onto the bed after her.

"Ikey hooky-nose!"

"Rodean snob!"

In the ensuing struggle, Diana forgot herself and rolled over onto Hy, knocking the breath out of him. "Oh, I *am* sorry, darling," Diana said tenderly.

"What?" Hy snarled, inflamed, whacking her in the ribs, beating her on the belly. "What?"

In the morning Hy, his mood masterful but lenient, thoughtfully provided a pillow for Diana. "For your butt," he said. Hy was eating his Fruitifort when the phone rang. He answered it, his voice thick: "Hullo."

"Hullo, Hy."

"Oh, it's you."

"Yeah. Did I wake you up? I can call back later."

"I'm up now. I could never fall asleep again. So just tell me what you want."

"I called to apologize."

"For what?"

"For last night."

"What did you do last night?"

"I'm sorry if anything I said gave you the impression – the erroneous impression – that, if it were the case, I would not be proud to be Jewish."

"What made you think that offended me?"

"Joyce. I told her she was imagining things."

"She certainly was. I can't think of anything you'd say that could offend me."

"Oh."

"And what ever gave you the screwy idea that I was touchy about being Jewish?"

"Oh, you know Joyce. She's hypersensitive."

"Okay, let's say I'm familiar with your sexually frustrated wife, but –"

"*My what wife?*"

"But what about you? I think you're being very condescending. I don't go for the idea of this phone call."

"Look, let's just forget anything happened last night. Now would you mind repeating what you said about my –"

"Nothing did happen last night. Except in the perversely racial-conscious mind of your wife."

"Hy, wait a minute. This is dreadful. I didn't call you up to quarrel. Tell you what. Why don't you and Diana come up for drinks tomorrow night? They're doing an old Gary Cooper Western on BBC-2."

"Some of us have better things to do at night than watch TV."

"Now what in the hell do you mean by that?"

"Skip it. Forget it."

"Gladly. Can we expect you tomorrow night, then?"

"Diana's coming down with the flu."

"Oh, I see. I see, old pal. Well, I do hope she feels better soon."

"Now what kind of a crack is that?"

"All I said was –"

"I heard you the first time, chickenshit. Thanks. I'll give her your heartfelt message."

"Well, that's very good of you. Now would you mind repeating what you said about my wi –"

"Goodbye," Hy said, and he hung up.

Mortimer shot an apprehensive glance at Joyce, smoking languorously at the breakfast table, her dressing gown falling open over her long coltish legs. Joyce was tall, with naturally curly brown hair, her breasts small. Okay, she's good-looking, radiating health in a windblown Canadian way, but she's not beautiful. She –

"How come," Joyce asked, "you have no Negroes on the editorial staff at Oriole Press?"

"*What?*"

Joyce lit a cigarette, inhaling with immense satisfaction.

"Because we've never had a Negro apply for an editorial job. Should I search Camden Town for one?"

"That would hardly be necessary. I could introduce you to one or two candidates."

Joyce worked for the Anti-Apartheid League. And Oxfam.

"Could you?"

"We never have any for dinner. It might make for a change, you know."

"Yes. Quite. Um, men or women? I mean that you could introduce me to."

"Oh, are you ever prejudiced! You're just a cesspool of received WASP ideas."

Doug, hearing their voices raised, suddenly stood at the kitchen door, beaming.

Four

NOTHING FLUSHED DOUG out of his room like a quarrel; he even tried to provoke them, for the truth was he had a gripe. Nearly all of Doug's fabulously rich classmates at Beatrice Webb House came from broken homes, which gave him reason to envy them. Take Neil Ferguson, for instance. He had been a nervy kid, a bed-wetter, until his parents were divorced two years ago, remarried almost immediately, and began to compete for Neil's affections. So that now, come the Easter hols, Neil could create traumas in two households while he vacillated between Bermuda with his mother and stepfather or Paris with his father and stepmother.

Doug was being misled, Mortimer knew, he was clearly better off in a happy – well, reasonably happy – home, but all the same Doug and two or three other Beatrice Webb boys felt deprived because they only had two parents each.

Damn that school, Mortimer thought.

No sooner had Mortimer driven Doug to school and turned into Regent's Park than he developed a puncture and had to change the tire himself. In the rain.

At Lloyd's bank, on Oxford Street, a day begun badly took an anguishing turn. Ahead of Mortimer in the queue there was an attractive, elegantly dressed girl. *Colored.* Now,

Mortimer was certainly not prejudiced, but even so he had to admit that the first thing he noticed about the attractive, elegantly dressed girl was that she was colored. When Mortimer had first entered the bank, there she was standing in the queue with *nobody behind her*. There were shorter queues leading to other tellers, there was even one teller with nobody to serve, but Mortimer, remembering Sharpsville, remembering Selma, Alabama, immediately fell in behind the attractive colored girl.

Well, she certainly was a jumpy one, obviously unsettled by his waiting behind her, possibly because there were now two other tellers with nobody to serve or maybe because he had edged too close behind her. Not that he could retreat a step now – that would be insulting. Finally the girl endorsed all her checks, eight of them, each made out for twenty-five pounds, handed them over (somewhat nervously, it seemed to Mortimer) and turned to go, which was when it happened. The attractive, elegantly dressed colored girl dropped one of her white gloves, and for an instant the two of them were suspended in time, like the frozen frame in a movie. Mortimer's first instinct was to retrieve her glove, but he checked it. She was, after all, colored, and he did not want her to think him condescending on the one hand, or sexually presumptuous on the other. And then her smile, a mere trace of a smile, was ambiguous. Was she waiting for him to retrieve the glove or was she amused by his dilemma? His ofay dilemma. Or perhaps she wasn't a militant and she thought it prejudiced of Mortimer not to retrieve the glove as he would have done instantly had she been white. Yes, he thought, that's it, but by this time she had scooped up the glove herself, cursing him in parting. "Mother-fucker," the elegantly dressed colored girl said; Mortimer was prepared to swear she called him mother-fucker.

But I'm not prejudiced, he thought, outraged. Scrutinizing

his own attitudes as honestly as possible, Mortimer felt (Joyce be damned) that he could objectively say of himself, coming out of Lloyd's bank on Oxford Street on a windy morning in October 1965, that, considering his small-town Ontario origins, his middle-class background, he was refreshingly free of prejudice. Even Ziggy Spicehandler would have to agree. Ziggy, he thought, how I miss him.

Joyce phoned him at the office. Before she could get a word out, he said, "If you ask me, almost all of Doug's problems can be traced to that bloody school."

"Would you rather that he was educated as you were?"

Mortimer had been to Upper Canada College. "I don't see why not."

"Full of repressions and establishment lies."

Establishment. Camp. WASP. She had all the bloody modish words.

"Well, I –"

"We'll discuss it later. Just please please don't be late for the rehearsal."

Mortimer had only been invited to the rehearsal for the Christmas play because he was in publishing and Dr. Booker, the founder, wanted Oriole to do a book about Beatrice Webb House. Drama was taught at the school by a Miss Lilian Tanner, who had formerly been with Joan Littlewood's bouncy group. A tall, willowy young lady, Miss Tanner wore her long black hair loose, a CND button riding her scrappy bosom. She assured Mortimer he was a most welcome visitor to her modest little workshop. Mortimer curled into a seat in the rear of the auditorium, trying to appear as unobtrusive as possible. He was only half attentive to begin with, reconciled to an afternoon of tedium larded with cuteness.

"We have a visitor this afternoon, class," Miss Tanner began sweetly. "Mr. Mortimer Griffin of Oriole Press."

Curly-haired heads, gorgeous pigtailed heads, whipped around, everybody giggly.

"Now all together, class . . ."

"*Good afternoon, Mr. Griffin.*"

Mortimer waved, unaccountably elated.

"Settle down now," Miss Tanner demanded, rapping her ruler against the desk. "Settle down, I said."

The class came to order.

"Now, this play that we are going to perform for the Christmas concert was written by . . . class?"

"A marquis!"

"Bang on!" Miss Tanner smiled, flushed with old-fashioned pride in her charges, and then she pointed her ruler at a rosy-cheeked boy. "What's a marquis, Tony?"

"What hangs outside the Royal Court Theatre."

"No, no, darling."

There were titters all around. Mortimer laughed himself, covering his mouth with his hand.

"That's a marquee. This is a marquis. A –"

A little girl bobbed up, waving her arms. Golden head, red ribbons. "A French nobleman!"

"Righty-ho! And what do we know about him . . . class?"

A boy began to jump up and down. Miss Tanner pointed her ruler at him.

"They put him in prison."

"Yes. Anybody know why?"

Everybody began to call out at once.

"Order! Order!" Miss Tanner demanded. "What ever will Mr. Griffin think of us?"

Giggles again.

"You have a go, Harriet. Why was the marquis put in prison?"

"Because he was absolutely super."

"Mmnn . . ."

"*And such a truth-teller.*"

"Yes. Any other reasons . . . Gerald?"

"Because the Puritans were scared of him."

"Correct. And what else do we know about the marquis?"

"Me, me!"

"No, me, miss. Please!"

"Eeny-meeny-miny-mo," Miss Tanner said, waving her ruler. "Catch a bigot by the toe . . . Frances!"

"That he was the freest spirit what ever lived."

"*Who* ever lived. Who, dear. And who said that?"

"Apollinaire."

"Jolly good. Anything else . . . Doug?"

"Um, he cut through the banality of everyday life."

"Indeed he did. And who said that?"

"Jean Genet."

"No."

"Hugh Hefner," another voice cried.

"Dear me, that's not even warm."

"Simone de Beauvoir."

"Right. And who is she?"

"A writer."

"Good. Very good. Anybody know anything else about the marquis?"

"He was in the Bastille and then in another place called Charenton."

"Yes. All together, class . . . Charenton."

"*Charenton.*"

"Anything else?"

Frances jumped up a again. "I know. Please, Miss Tanner. Please, me."

"Go ahead, darling."

"He had a very, very, very big member."

"Yes indeed. And –"

But now Frances's elder brother, Jimmy, leaped to his feet, interrupting. "Like Mummy's new friend," he said.

Shrieks. Laughter. Miss Tanner's face reddened. For the first time she stamped her foot. "Now I don't like that, Jimmy. I don't like that one bit."

"Sorry, Miss Tanner."

"That's tittle-tattle, isn't it?"

"Yes, Miss Tanner."

"We mustn't tittle-tattle on one another here."

"Sorry . . ."

"And now," Miss Tanner said, stepping up to the blackboard, "can anyone give me another word for member?"

"*Cock*," came a little girl's shout; and Miss Tanner wrote it down.

"Beezer."

"*Pwick.*"

"Male organ."

"*Penis.*"

"Hard-on."

Miss Tanner looked dubious. She frowned. "Not always," she said, and she didn't write it down.

"*Fucking-machine.*"

"*Putz.*"

"You're being sectarian again, Monty," Miss Tanner said, somewhat irritated.

"Joy stick."

A pause.

"Anybody else?" Miss Tanner asked.

"Hot rod."

"Mmn. Dodgy," Miss Tanner said, but she wrote it down on the blackboard, adding a question mark. "Anybody else?"

"Yes," a squeaky voice cried, now that her back was turned. "Tea-kettle."

Miss Tanner whirled around, outraged. "*Who said that?*" she demanded.

Silence.

"Well, I never. I want to know who said that. *Immediately.*"

No answer.

"Very well, then. No rehearsal," she said, sitting down and tapping her foot. "We are simply going to sit here and sit here and sit here until who ever said that owns up."

Nothing.

"I'm sorry about this fuck-up, Mr. Griffin. It's most embarrassing."

Mortimer shrugged.

"I'm waiting, class."

Finally a fat squinting boy came tearfully to his feet. "It was me, Miss Tanner," he said in a small voice. "I said tea-kettle."

"Would you be good enough to tell us why, Reggie?"

"When my nanny . . . I mean my little brother's nanny, um, takes us, ah, out . . ."

"Speak up, please."

"When my nanny takes me, um, us . . . to Fortnum's for tea, well, before I sit down she always asks us do we, do" – Reggie's head hung low; he paused, swallowing his tears – "do I have to water my tea-kettle."

"Well. Well, well. I see," Miss Tanner said severely. "Class, can anyone tell me what Reggie's nanny is?"

"A prude!"

"Repressed!"

"Victorian!"

"All together now."

"*Reggie's nanny is a dry cunt!*"

"She is against . . . class?"

"Life force."

"And?"

"Pleasure!"

"Right. *And truth-sayers.* Remember that. Because it's sexually repressed bitches like Reggie's nanny who put truth-sayers like the marquis in prison."

The class was enormously impressed.

"May I sit down now?" Reggie asked.

"Sit down, what?"

"Sit down, please, Miss Tanner?"

"Yes, Reggie. You may sit down."

At which point Mortimer slipped out of the rear exit of the auditorium, without waiting to see a run-through of the play. Without even finding out what play they were doing.

Five

"SELF-EXPRESSION BE damned," Mortimer shouted. "This is his last term at that mockery of a school. I'm taking him out."

"*You're* taking him out? Doug is my child."

"Ours."

"I carried him. This is the twentieth century, darling, not the nineteenth. Any decision as to Doug's education will be made jointly."

"All right, then, jointly. But –"

"You'd better hurry or you'll be late."

Naturally Joyce had begged off. She wouldn't miss *Insult*, the new BBC-2 interview program. So Mortimer had to lie to Miss Ryerson. He said they couldn't get a baby-sitter.

"I *am* sorry," Miss Ryerson said.

Too late Mortimer discovered that the farce he and Miss Ryerson had settled on for Tuesday night starred the West End's most talked-about leading lady, the incomparable Mr. Danny La Rue.

Afterwards Mortimer acquiesced to Agnes Laura Ryerson's high-spirited request for a pub crawl. Mortimer took her to Dirty Dick's. She was enthralled with The Prospect of Whitby. But, alas, they ended up at a pub in Victoria, where burly six-foot Guardsmen habitually came to take more shillings, serving other queens. Mortimer devoutly hoped that Agnes Laura Ryerson was too innocent to comprehend the nature of the transactions going on around them, between Household Troopers and the flushed, affluent men who were buying them drinks. Miss Ryerson generously stood two of Her Majesty's Guards to a round herself. "Here's to the thin red line," she said, raising her glass.

This made one of the Guardsmen chuckle. "Oh, my dear," he said to his beribboned comrade, "did you hear that?"

Enough is enough, Mortimer told Joyce when he finally got home. "My only hope," he added wearily, "is that Miss Ryerson returns to Canada with at least one of her illusions intact."

"I couldn't care less," Joyce said, irritated.

"Well now," Mortimer asked in his nastiest voice, "how was *Insult?* Groovy?"

"Mn. Not bad."

Joyce was absolutely in touch, thoroughly with it. Unlike me, Mortimer thought.

Unlike me.

His missing *Insult* tonight was typical; for he gathered from her self-satisfied expression that it was going to be the rage. A thingee. Like TW 3. Keeping up exhausted and baffled Mortimer. He wasn't totally uninformed, but his timing was badly off. Not that Joyce helped. Oh, no. The bitch let him go on reading Bernard Levin long after he had gone out of fashion. Then there was the case of Kenneth Tynan. He remembered very well how she had used to quote his theater reviews. Well, how was he supposed to know that you were not to read his *film* reviews? Mortimer quoted one of his film reviews at a party once and Joyce gave him that special look of hers. "Tynan is fifties," she said. Like her favorite coffee bar of that decade, The Partisan.

"Would you care for a drink?" Joyce asked.

"I'm going to have a bath first."

Mortimer, forty-two years old now, was still slender. He

suffered no protruding belly and his hair had not yet begun to gray or recede. His features were regular. Yes, he had to admit, considering himself in the bathroom mirror, yes, yes, the sour truth is I'm tall and handsome. Conventionally handsome, as Joyce said again and again with unconcealed repugnance. Like the old-style movie stars. Gable, Taylor, Tyrone Power. An unused face, he had once heard Ziggy Spicehandler say. Clean-cut, he might have added, unmistakably WASP, like the smiling, sincere husband in the unit trust advertisements on whose forehead ran the slogan: "Investor at 35, capitalist at 60."

Shit. Look at you. Just look at you, Griffin.

Ziggy Spicehandler, to whom he owed so much, had been the first to make him realize how truly repulsive he was. "Man," he had said affectionately, tauntingly, pinching his cheek, "you look like one of those male models. You know, getting out of a sports car in the *Esquire* ads."

Ziggy himself was short, hirsute, barrel-chested. His hooky nose had been twice broken and he had a thick neck and waxy tangled hairs protruded from his jug ears. His fingernails were black, there were warts on his broad square hands, and you could tell, just looking at him, that in other people's houses he filled his pockets with cigarettes and peed without lifting the seat. Women found Ziggy Spicehandler exciting. Wherever he went, even at the most modish parties, they turned to look at him. Me, Mortimer thought, I can stand alone at a party for hours, nobody turns to look at me.

No. Once a sexy young girl had come up to him, "Well hullo there," she had said a little drunkenly.

"Hello yourself."

Swaying, she said, "You must be in advertising."

"I beg your pardon?"

"Well, you should be. You've got the face."

Suburban, she meant. Ziggy, on the other hand, had an anti-suburban face.

The last time Ziggy had come to stay with them, Doug had been three. Ziggy, to Joyce's amazement, seemed to adore the child, and offered to baby-sit time and again. He played ball with Doug on the Heath. Twice weekly he also took him to Regent's Park Zoo, unfortunately timing these visits to coincide with feeding time in the reptile house, a matter of fascination to Ziggy. Doug was just learning how to talk then and Ziggy took him happily in hand.

"Apeman," he would say, pointing out a priest to him; and he instructed him to say "kiss my ass," fortunately coming out "kis'mas," for "thank you." To begin with, Joyce was baffled by Doug's choice of words, but actually the boy was even more confused, for what Joyce taught him to call "nun" in the afternoon, Ziggy insisted was "baggy tits" in the evening.

Inevitably Joyce discovered that far from being retarded, Doug was being perversely misled by Ziggy, and this led to a scorching quarrel with Mortimer. A volte-face sort of quarrel, Mortimer, rather than Joyce, finding himself unwillingly defending the new. While Ziggy, he admitted, was behaving irresponsibly, she must understand that he was not sadistic. He truly believed that our parents had raised us on nothing but lies and to be untaught, so to speak, was the only way of liberating a child. Thereby leading him, as Ziggy would put it, toward a state of grace. Even so, Mortimer had to agree that it was off-putting and he regretfully prepared to tell Ziggy he must leave the house.

It never came to that. One day Joyce sent Ziggy to Dr. Schneider to pick up a prescription for her. Schneider, an overworked man, was in the habit of leaving prescriptions to be called for in a box on his outside steps. This, Ziggy discovered, was a fairly common labor-saving practice among National Health doctors. On a good day, riffling through prescriptions left outside here, there, and everywhere, he was able to accumulate a very nice supply of pills with an appreciable morphine or opiate content. This was immensely gratifying to Ziggy, who was not getting sufficient stuff from his own doctor, a sour Puritan; it also enabled him to acquire much-needed cash by selling his surplus pills to others in need. Eventually the police cottoned on to the traffic and began to keep a watch on Hampstead surgeries. Ziggy left for Paris.

Coming out of the bathroom, Mortimer asked Joyce, "Why do women find Ziggy Spicehandler so attractive?"

"I don't."

Liar.

"But," she continued, "I'd say it's that he has the face of a man who has visited the darker regions of hell and come back again."

Mortimer grunted and flicked on the TV set to catch the late news. He was in time for the last item. The Star Maker, the newscaster said, would not comment on recent rumors that he was about to transfer his headquarters from Las Vegas to London. But earlier today he had made a successful takeover bid for a London publishing house, Oriole Press. In some quarters, especially in the City, the newscaster went on to say, this was taken as an indicator of future intentions. Then the Star Maker's emblem was flashed briefly on the screen.

Two snakes coupling.

Six

THE AGELESS, UNDYING Star Maker, about whom almost nothing was known, almost everything was rumor, vile rumor. Whose very sex had recently become a hotly debated issue. Some said he was a man, others insisted he was turning into a woman; a few, astoundingly enough, whispered that something even more sinister was in the offing. The Star Maker. Imagine, Mortimer thought, Oriole Press passing into such obscene hands.

Naturally the publishing scene, like everything else, had changed considerably since Mortimer had first come to London fifteen years ago. There had been failures, regroupings, and, above all, a plethora of American takeovers. But Mortimer had believed that Oriole Press, with its unequaled traditions, inadequate gas fires, antique filing system and tea rings, was inviolate. Now, without warning, the saintly Lord Woodcock had surrendered control, obviously to avoid death duties, Mortimer reflected, and overnight Oriole Press had become possibly the most insignificant unit in the Star Maker's international business empire.

Horrifying. But on second thought Mortimer wondered if this was not another typically shrewd ploy by Lord Woodcock. The Star Maker, his interests global, swooped out of the sky one day to settle a strike on a Malayan opium farm and the next day flew on to Rome, perhaps, to fire the director on one of his multimillion-dollar film productions. His interests were so vast and all-embracing, taking in film and TV production companies, airlines, newspapers, diamond mines, oil refineries and gambling casinos, that he was bound to take no notice of Oriole Press. We're no more than a bauble, Mortimer thought, feeling considerably better, a prestigious trinket. Our turnover is too pathetically small to interest such a Goliath.

Only an hour later the first of the Star Maker's legendary idea men arrived. A team of efficiency experts had flown in from Frankfort and Lord Woodcock, making one of his rare appearances at Oriole House, came round to introduce them. There was Herr Dr. Manheim and his three secretaries. Two of them were laconic men, obsessive note-takers who wore black leather coats. The third, Fräulein Ringler, was a rather comely young lady, even taking the dueling scar on her cheek into account.

Unfortunately the very first meeting with the efficiency team got off to a bad start.

Mortimer's secretary, shy, unobtrusive Miss Fishman, who had worked at Oriole ever since shortly after the war when she came to England out of a displaced-persons camp, suddenly seized a letter opener and fell on Fräulein Ringler, scratching, biting, and stabbing. It took Mortimer and Hy to pull her off Fräulein Ringler and drag her into another office.

"Dear, dear," Lord Woodcock said.

Lord Woodcock, Mortimer could see, was dismayed. Obviously. The saintly old man's credo was "We must love one another or die"; and he lived by it. Soon after the war Mr. Woodcock, as he was then, had collected case histories and compiled a book, elegantly produced if necessarily slender, about all the charitable little acts done by Germans to Jews during the Nazi era. Here a simple but good-hearted sergeant offering spoonfuls of marmalade to Jewish children before they were led off to the gas chambers, somewhere else a fabled general refusing to drink with Eichmann or a professor quoting Heine right to a Nazi's face.

"What is it, child?" Lord Woodcock asked,

"The necklace she's wearing," Miss Fishman said, still panting. "It's my mother's. Before that it belonged to my grandmother."

Miss Fishman's mother, who had been roasted in the ovens of Treblinka, as had every other member of her family, was not merely another dry Jewish statistic, altogether too horrific, as they say, for the ordinary imagination to cope with. Miss Fishman's mother was in fact the one-millionth Jew to be burned, not counting half or quarter Jews or babies who weighed under nine pounds before being flung into the ovens. This made for a very, very special occasion, and in honor of it Miss Fishman's mother was accorded treatment quite out of the ordinary. For her burning the furnace chambers of Treblinka were festooned with flowers and gaily colored Chinese lanterns. Just as today's presidents and prime ministers will sign historical documents with as many as thirty pens, passing them out as souvenirs, so Mrs. Fishman's gold fillings and other valuables were divided among extermination quota leaders from various concentration camps, who had been invited to Treblinka for the day. Thus, the burning of the one-millionth was one of the most ring-a-ding nights in the history of the Third Reich and to this day – the Star Maker himself assured Mortimer, once he got to know him – it is commemorated by survivors of that sentimental barbecue wherever they may be.

"The necklace belongs to my mother," Miss Fishman insisted over and over again.

"But," Lord Woodcock chided her gently, "Fräulein Ringler was merely a child at the time, and so even if the necklace did once belong to your mother, a dubious possibility, then she certainly can't be considered culpable."

"I don't care, I don't care," Miss Fishman shouted, stamping her foot childishly. "Let me at her, the German bitch. I'll kill her."

"German bitch?" Now Lord Woodcock, not one to lose his temper, actually raised his voice and banged his cane against the floor. "What are you?" he demanded, appalled. "A racist?"

"No."

"A grudgy type, then?"

Thus reproached, Miss Fishman began to sob brokenly.

"I'm afraid, child, that your outburst has reminded me of nothing more than Nazi ravings, both in tone and attitude."

"I'm unworthy," Miss Fishman moaned.

Lord Woodcock took her arm, the one with the number tattooed on it, and began to stroke it. "It was Nazi doctrine," he continued soothingly, "wasn't it, to assume national guilt, to assume that it pertains equally to all individuals, and to visit upon the young the presumed sins of their elders."

"Forgive me," she pleaded.

"Meditate, if you will, my child, upon the fate of the Canaanites and Amalekites, and you will see that the extermination of nations is not new. I especially recommend I Samuel 15:3: 'and spare them not; but slay both man and woman, infant and suckling.' " Still patting her arm he whispered, "so it is not for the Jewish people, beloved as they are to me, to cast the first stone or to judge. Is it, my child?"

Mortimer helped Miss Fishman out of her chair. "Thank you," she said, smiling at him.

"You're welcome," Lord Woodcock said, and then he unlocked the office door, paused, and turned to smile beneficently on Miss Fishman, the light from behind illuminating his massive head. "Remember this too, child. Like you, Fräulein Ringler was born to die alone."

Miss Fishman stared at Lord Woodcock's retreating figure. "He's a saint," she said.

Yes, Mortimer thought, recalling his first deep conversation with Lord Woodcock. The time Mortimer had told him that when he had been with the Canadian army in Germany, immediately after the war, he had expected that they were in for a bloodbath. Mortimer had thought, he explained, that Jewish officers and men in the allied armies would run amok, shooting down Germans indiscriminately or at least hunting down former SS men and hanging them from lamp-posts, but in the western sector acts of vengeance had been scarce, Mortimer told Lord Woodcock, and he had not known of one that was Jewish-inspired.

Lord Woodcock had nodded; he had smiled. "It would not have done," he explained, "for my Jewish brothers to respond to animal behavior with yet another obscenely animal act."

Then he told Mortimer how after the war was done but still a festering wound, he and his followers, a number of saintly Jews among them, had traveled to Germany to demonstrate to the world how love, and only love, could conquer hatred. They had cleared the rubble from the bombed parks and filled in the shell-torn fields. They had planted acres of wheat and corn and orchards and botanical gardens, heedless of scoffing onlookers who had said nothing would grow where the old men and their students had sown. Nothing would grow, they had said, because these men, however well-intentioned, were totally lacking in agricultural acumen. Something else. They were sweetly bound by such reverence for life that they would not tolerate chemical fertilizers or sprays. But the gardens and fields and orchards bloomed, bloomed miraculously, flowers and fruit trees and wheat proliferating in such abundance that it seemed to some that God above must have blessed the seedlings. Of course the knockers said no; they rudely pointed out that underneath the meadows and parks of Germany there ran the most rare and nourishing of fertilizers – rivers of human blood and mashed bone and burned flesh. This fertilizer in fact was said to be so enduring that to this day, according to the experts, it accounted for the incomparably succulent asparagus of the Schwartzwald and the recent fecund years enjoyed by the vineyards of the Rhine, thereby bringing dividends to gourmets the world over, regardless of race, color or creed.

Seven

DINO TOMASSO, FAT, oily-skinned, and short of breath, disgusted Mortimer. He also astonished him. The new man, Mortimer and the other editors were told, had been flown over from Hollywood to goose Oriole's list, regardless of the fact, Mortimer complained acrimoniously, that it was already the envy of most other London publishing houses. Tomasso, a keep-fit fanatic, did push-ups on his office carpet every morning, which was somewhat staggering, considering that his right leg, beginning above the knee, was artificial, and he was missing two fingers from his left hand. He also owned a pair of impossibly thick pebble glasses, which were always close at hand. Yet he didn't wear them for reading. Or driving. In fact he hardly ever put them on.

Tomasso had only been with Oriole for two days when, acting on a brief prepared by the efficiency team from Frankfort, he inaugurated a new series of books at Oriole Press: the Our Living History biographies. Then, without warning, Tomasso began to process existing staff and hire new people, applying the Star Maker's seemingly wayward methods. This meant that Mortimer, like everyone else who worked for the Star Maker, had to submit to an exhaustive health check. Fortunately, he passed. So did Hy Rosen. But John Cameron, Oriole's likable sales chief, was released because he had a mild heart condition. "But Cameron's been with us for years," Mortimer protested, outraged. "His condition doesn't interfere with his work."

"The Star Maker," Tomasso said, "cannot tolerate ill health among his people."

New staff had to undergo metabolism and blood tests, ECG's, and other trying ordeals. Even secretaries were X-rayed and offered work based on their physical well-being, not their shorthand speed, the best positions going to those girls willing to sign an undertaking that they would undergo a hysterectomy if the management deemed it necessary. Among the new staff there was one Polly Morgan, a picture of good health. "Polly is headed for big things here," Tomasso said, studying the doctor's charts.

"Oh," Mortimer said coldly.

"She is the same blood type as the Star Maker. Very rare, that."

This made Mortimer laugh.

"You know, I've been with the Star Maker, Blessed Be His Name, for twenty-five years now. Started out as an assistant script editor, the coffee boy. What would you say, Griffin, if I told you that he hired me in the first place because he liked the color of my eyes?"

"You said *he*," Mortimer said.

Tomasso waited, amused.

"There are rumors that – well, he's a woman."

"That's all for this morning, Griffin."

God damn it, Tomasso thought, he'll bear watching, that one. I knew it.

Somewhat baffled, Mortimer returned to his office to brood. Actually, he was put off but not worried about Tomasso for he confidently expected that his first new project, the ill-conceived Our Living History series, would be a costly flop and thereafter, he assumed, Tomasso would depart, leaving them to muddle through as in the old days.

Mortimer and Hy, it developed, were not allowed to commission biographies for the new series, the orders had to originate in Frankfort, which was insulting, but also advantageous: if the first two biographies – the pilots, Tomasso called them – had remaindered written all over them, they couldn't be blamed. The first biography was of a Labour politician, once a firebrand but today a bore almost unknown to the public, and the second was of a once-well-known film star who hadn't worked since 1945.

The first morning editorial conference called by Tomasso was stiff and formal. At the second, he introduced his idea of a Cinemagicians series; and all at once the old editorial hands looked forward to nothing so much as a conference called to consider titles for this series, if only because the puzzling, somewhat abstracted Polly Morgan had been put in charge.

Polly was a bewitchingly gorgeous young thing, whose every gesture, however innocently intended, was maddeningly sexy. And distracting. Not that she could be blamed, Mortimer felt, if, pondering an idea, her lips slightly parted, tapping a pencil against her teeth, she made for an untimely ache in the groin for all the men at the conference. Neither could she be legitimately reproached because discussion would suddenly falter when she was so enthused over a project as not to notice that her skirt had ridden up; a distraction compounded by the fact that Polly sat on a high art department stool and all the other editors, anticipating this excruciating delight, swiftly took to arranging themselves on sofas so that, dependent on their proclivities, Polly's legs or adorable bottom was at eye level.

All of which, Mortimer felt, was insulting to Polly who had, to his delight, turned out to be highly skilled and most knowledgeable about films.

At a morning conference, about a week after Tomasso had come to Oriole Press, he turned from a discussion of pending

Cinemagician titles to consider the manuscript of a new novel. "Who's this kid's editor?" he asked.

Hy beamed, his hand shooting up.

"I want to talk to you about this manuscript after lunch," Tomasso said. "That's all for this morning, fellas."

Mortimer caught up with Hy in the hall. "Well," he said, "what about lunch at The Eight Bells?"

"Not me," Hy said, his manner truculent.

So Mortimer went on to lunch alone. Hy lingered in his office until he was certain the editorial floor had emptied and then, taking a portfolio of photographs with him, he went off in search of Polly Morgan, whom he hoped to interest in an idea of his own for the Cinemagicians series.

Polly, just as Hy had anticipated, was alone in the design department. No phones rang. No typewriters clattered. Coming up behind her, as she bent over a drawing board, Hy was concerned lest he startle her, so he coughed and said, "It's frightfully quiet in here."

Polly whirled around, her eyes widening. "Too quiet," she said. "I don't like it."

Hy smiled and turned to set down his portfolio when suddenly Polly let out a piercing scream.

"But I'm not going to touch you. I'm Jewish."

Polly shrieked again.

"What's the matter with you?"

Again and again she shrieked and Hy, alarmed, fled the design department and bolted out of Oriole House, across Soho Square, down Frith Street, not stopping until he reached The Eight Bells, where he instantly ordered a large brandy.

"Anything wrong?" Mortimer asked, concerned.

No, no, Hy protested, but he looked sickly and after lunch he seemed loath to return to Oriole House.

And small wonder, Mortimer reflected afterwards, for no sooner did they emerge from the lift on the editorial floor than Polly came tottering out of the design department, her lovely black hair disarrayed and her blouse ripped open, revealing a handful of white lace bra and breast.

As Mortimer stood there, aghast, Hy seemed about to flee. Which was when Polly staggered into his arms. "Without you," she said breathlessly, "I would have been a goner for sure."

Hy gaped.

"I feel much better now that it's over," Polly said, kissing him. "Do you feel better now?"

"Yes," Hy stammered, hastily extricating himself from Polly's embrace. "Yes, I do."

Tomasso summoned Mortimer to his office.

"Um, we ought to get to know each other, don't you think?"

"Surely," Mortimer said uneasily.

"Sit down. Relax."

Mortimer sat down. He waited.

"What brand of poison do you prefer?"

"Scotch, if you don't mind?"

"It's my pleasure."

Tomasso served the drinks, but still Mortimer sat silent and unyielding. Tomasso scratched his head, searching for an icebreaker. Finally, inspired, he beamed and asked, "Getting much?"

"I beg your pardon?"

"Well, me, I've got the hots for Polly Morgan. Does she put out, Mort?"

"I wouldn't know. Furthermore, if that's why you asked me into your office –"

"Hell, no." Tomasso bit his lip. He cracked his knuckles. "Say, what do you think of the poetry of Mao Tse-tung?"

"I wouldn't know. I'm unfamiliar with it."

"Me too. You see," he said, smiling, "we have something in common after all."

"Have we?"

"You strike me as a very human being, Mort."

"Thank you."

"Say, you know what the Star Maker once said to me about Senator McCarthy? He said, quote, The Senator was more than a politician. He was the most effective film critic of his time. He did more than Agee or *Cahiers du Cinéma* to clean the liberal hacks out of Hollywood."

"Does that mean," Mortimer asked indignantly, "that the Star Maker admired Senator McCarthy?"

"The Star Maker," Tomasso said, "admires nobody, except . . ." He wavered.

"Yes?"

"Well, there was a certain historical figure. The Chevalier d'Éon, a French nobleman. He first turned up at court dressed as a broad, trying to steal Louis XV from Madame de Pompadour. When Louis discovered this new piece was really a drag artist he didn't blow his top. He made the Chevalier a trusted diplomat. Once, in 1775, I think, he sent him to Russia on a secret mission disguised as a niece of his official agent. The next year the Chevalier d'Éon returned to Russia dressed as a man to finish his mission. Kinky, huh?"

"Yes."

"One for the road?" Tomasso asked, grabbing Mortimer's glass.

"If you like."

While Tomasso went to refill the glasses, Mortimer, unaware that he was being watched, picked up the thick pebble spectacles on the desk and tried them. To his amazement, he discovered that they were not made of optical lenses at all. They were plain glass.

"Here's looking at you," Tomasso said.

"Cheers."

As soon as Mortimer had gone, Tomasso put through a call to Frankfort. "I want somebody to check out Griffin for me," he said. "The complete background. You can start by getting me his army records."

Eight

THE NEXT MORNING, Saturday, Mortimer received a copy of a magazine called *Jewish Thought* in the mail. Attached was a printed note, WITH THE COMPLIMENTS OF THE EDITOR, and underneath, penned with a lavish hand, "*Respectfully, J. Shalinsky.*" J. Shalinsky? J. Shalinsky's editorial dealt searchingly with the dilemma of the Jewish artist in a philistine society. The lead article by I. M. Sinclair, M.A. (Leeds), was titled "The Anti-Semite as an Intellectual: A Study of the Novels of Graham Greene." Another article by Lionel Gold, M.D., was titled "Diaspora IX – On Being a Reform Jew in Hampstead Garden Suburb." There were numerous book reviews, two sentimental poems translated from the Yiddish, and a maudlin Israeli short story.

"What are you laughing at?" Joyce called out from the kitchen.

Mortimer showed her the magazine. "Don't you find it ludicrous?"

"No."

There was a knock at the door. "I'll get it," Mortimer said.

It was the lachrymose little man, the puny round-shouldered man with horn-rimmed spectacles, who was attending Mortimer's lectures. "You got the magazine?" he asked.

"My wife. Um, Mr. . . ."

"Shalinsky, Jacob Shalinsky."

"Good morning," Joyce said. "Coffee?"

"If it's no trouble I'd prefer a cuppa. So," Shalinsky asked, turning to Mortimer, "what do you think?"

"I think it's bloody presumptuous of you to show up here unannounced at this hour and –"

"No, no, no. About the magazine."

"But it just came. I haven't had time to look at it yet."

"If you don't like it all you have to do is tell me why. No evasions, please. Don't beat around the bush."

"Tea will be ready in a minute," Joyce said.

"Ta." Shalinsky set his homburg down on a chair.

"If there's anything else she can get you," Mortimer said, "just ask and –"

"Eggs would be nice. Sunny side up."

"Look here, Shalinsky. This is not a restaurant. You can't –"

"Mortimer," Joyce said.

"It's not like I came empty-handed," Shalinsky said quickly. "I have something for you."

Mortimer watched while Shalinsky unwrapped his parcel thinking, you can keep your Goddamn chopped liver, thank you, and I don't want this apartment stinking of shmaltz herring. Shalinsky rolled the string into a ball and dropped it into his pocket. The brown wrapping paper, already worn and wrinkled, he folded into eight and put into another pocket. Revealed was no herring but a de luxe edition of color plates by Marc Chagall.

"It occurred to me," he said, "that a bloke so interested in Kafka might also find beauty in the art of Marc Chagall."

"What a lovely book, Mortimer!"

"You keep out of this."

"Would you be willing," Shalinsky asked, "to write a review . . . a little appreciation . . . of this book for the next issue of *Jewish Thought*?"

Mortimer hesitated.

"We pay our contributors, of course. Not much, but –"

"That's not the point."

But with a shrewd eye on Joyce, he continued, "And this smashing – and need I say, *very* expensive – book would be yours. That goes without saying."

"Yes, but –"

"Of course Mortimer will do it. Why, he's honored."

Nine

Mortimer had just settled in behind his desk on Monday morning, and turned to his correspondence, when Daphne Humber-Guest showed up unannounced and troubled to chat about her novel-in-progress.

Daphne was twenty-five. Big and bulging, toothy, with a formidable jaw and a long tangle of greasy brown hair tumbling to her sloped shoulders. Everything about her was askew. Even her juglike breasts, looking outwards, seemed to droop in different directions. Ill-advisedly she wore a tight sweater and a miniskirt. As she heaved her enormous bottom into a chair, taking a breath before she crossed her legs, Daphne's knees loomed up at Mortimer like apple pies.

Among the literary lionesses who were making London a Saigon of the Sex War, Daphne's name was writ large. She had first made her mark by keeping and then publishing a decidedly unprudish journal of the breakup of her marriage, which very quickly hit the best-seller lists. Queried by reporters about an especially outrageous passage in the journal, she said, "I cannot invent. I must know everything I write about firsthand."

Fame did not agree with Daphne, it made her melancholy, she said, and for months on end she was photographed by all the glossy magazines looking lonely even at the most crowded parties. Then Ziggy Spicehandler, giving London another whirl at the time, burst into her life, and the newspapers began to run photographs of the young couple, obviously entranced with each other, as seen here, there, and everywhere. They were, they said, not going to marry, but instead would live together, which didn't seem to especially interest anybody until, at a hastily called press conference, Ziggy revealed that they would be living together *openly*.

"Even so," a gossip columnist said, "there isn't much of a story in it."

Two other columnists stood up and reached for their coats.

"Fuck. Shit. Piss. Cock," Ziggy shouted. "Let's see you print that, you emasculated bastards."

Another reporter headed for the door. Which was when Daphne, clutching Ziggy to her, said, "In spite of all I feel for him, I still practice self-abuse."

"Me too," Ziggy hollered.

Now representatives from the pop newspapers began to drift out. But reporters from the quality newspapers perked up, sensing something that went beyond gossip. An issue.

"I excite myself," Daphne said, "with photographs of naked men."

"I use photos of naked chicks," Ziggy said, "but it doesn't work for me . . . *unless they're black*."

The man from the *Guardian* instantly took out his notebook.

"But even D. H. Lawrence," another reporter said, "was against masturbation."

"D. H. Lawrence," Daphne said, "never gave a thought to others. I'm sure I don't need to masturbate. I've got lovers to spare."

"Me too," Ziggy said.

"But what about the ugly people of this world?" Daphne asked. "The herd? The people who can't get a table at Alvaro's?"

"The girls who can't afford Vidal Sassoon?"

"What about the cripples?"

"The albinos, what about them, man?"

"Would you deny those who can't readily find sexual partners what might be their only sexual outlet?"

Before anyone could answer, Daphne added, tears welling in her eyes, "Think of the men locked up in prison."

"And women."

"And what about the hospitals?"

"And old people's homes?"

"Lepers."

"Basket cases."

This brought an alert reporter to his feet. "Basket cases," he said.

"Oh, all right then," Daphne said. "Be niggly."

"You cats haven't got any poetry in you at all. You're fact-bound."

Mortimer, among others, was pleased for Daphne; Ziggy would be good for her, he thought, an education, but just a week later came the bitter split. It seems Daphne was well into her first draft of *The Totally Honest Affair* before she discovered that Ziggy had already sold the film rights, based on a synopsis. Outsiders, pinched, unperceptive bystanders, were critical of Ziggy's behavior; so in fact was Mortimer. Then Ziggy took Mortimer aside to explain the convoluted but true meaning of what he had done. His purpose, he said, had been twofold. By pulling the rug out, so to speak, from under Daphne's journal-in-progress, he was saving her from repeating herself artistically. By selling the synopsis for a large fee, but never turning in a screenplay, he demonstrated to commercial film makers that he could not be bought.

Daphne, unfortunately, did not see it that way. Swearing never to trust a man again, she tore up her manuscript. She began work on an unsentimental novel about the rise of a lovely working-class Yorkshire model girl, badly used, sexually used, by scheming sophisticated London editors, painters, writers, actors and other depraved types. In the end the gorgeous girl marries an aging duke, she acquires wealth and a title, but inside, *Where She Lives*, she is empty.

"You have no idea," she said to Mortimer, "the trouble I'm having, how work on this novel is exhausting me." She went on to explain how her mother, the most narrow-minded of County conservatives, had come to London unannounced, found her in bed with two Negroes, and instantly jumped to conclusions. "One way or another," Daphne said, "this bloody novel is taking all my time."

No sooner did Mortimer get rid of Daphne than he ran into Hy in the hall.

"Oh, Hy, you and Diana are coming with us to *Different* tomorrow night, aren't you?"

"Wouldn't you be embarrassed? Being seen with a Jew?"

"Look, Hy, it's going to be *the* event of the festival. People are falling over themselves trying to get tickets. You know that."

"Get stuffed." Then, as an afterthought, Hy added with implied menace, "Major," before he turned and ambled off, arms hanging loose, fingers flexing, as if the hall were a ring and he were retiring to his own corner after a grueling but stirring round. His round.

Busted major, he could have said. *Had anybody heard?* No. All the same it was the first reference Hy, who knew all about it, had made to the war in years and it was enough to unnerve Mortimer. The bloody war. As things stood, girls such as Polly Morgan and Daphne Humber-Guest were probably convinced that he was a bore, essentially prudish, but there was still, he dared to hope, an underlying respect; i.e., a friend of Ziggy Spicehandler's couldn't be all bad, but if . . .

Polly Morgan! What did he care what she thought? I don't. Neither am I attracted to her. Why, it doesn't even bear thinking about, Mortimer decided.

After work Mortimer took a taxi to the Prince Albert Hotel, armed with flowers and chocolates and the newspapers. Miss Ryerson looked small and pale. Not well within herself, as she might say. Mortimer drank coffee with her, he talked to her soothingly, and together they watched television. Paul McCartney joked about his M.B.E. Peter Cook recited a Betjeman-like poem celebrating the public conveniences of yesteryear. Mortimer hastily switched to the commercial channel, catching a Jesuit who was debating with a psychiatrist whether or not Jesus Christ had had carnal knowledge of Mary and, come to think of it, Martha as well. Switching back to the BBC, Mortimer was relieved to find Kenneth Tynan's face filling the screen. Then, just as Mortimer was explaining to Miss Ryerson that not since GBS had served as a critic had London known such a dazzling reviewer, such a master of language, Tynan said it. The word.

"Holy mackerel! Did he just say," Miss Ryerson asked, "did that fella just say f-dash-dash-k?"

"There's something wrong with the set," Mortimer said, diving for the dial.

"Shoot. Mortimer, I want you to check me out of this hotel instantly. This is not what I expected of London."

Mortimer nodded understandingly, gloomily. "Are you going home, then?"

"My goodness, no. I want you to find me what is called a bed-sitter, I think."

"What?" Mortimer said, forgetting himself so far as to light a cigarette.

"Mortimer Griffin, I've had quite enough for one week without you lighting a cigarette in my room."

"Sorry."

"I'm going to stay right here and teach."

Before Mortimer could comment, she shot him a defiant look and said, "England needs me."

England needs me. Mortimer was reminded of those

wartime cartoons that showed a bulldog-like Winston Churchill rolling up his sleeves. "You know," he said, bursting with affection, "You may have something there."

"Then you'll help me?"

Yes, he nodded, and he took Miss Ryerson to Rule's for dinner. A special treat.

"I don't believe for one minute," Miss Ryerson said, "what that big ignorant black man said."

"I beg your pardon," Mortimer said, flushing.

"We are most decidedly not done for. My goodness, the last loudmouth to make that mistake was Hitler."

"Yes, Miss Ryerson."

The waiter brought them each a plate of smoked trout. Absently, Mortimer picked up his fork.

"Hold your horses," Miss Ryerson said.

Immediately Mortimer understood. Embarrassed, yet somehow proud, he bowed his head.

"Dear Lord, for what we are about to receive," Miss Ryerson began, "we now give thanks . . ."

Ten

UNLIKE OTHER FILM festival presentations, *Different* was being shown almost secretively in a small theater, appropriately underground. The fabled hairdresser was there; so were the anointed model girls and actors, the legendary photographer, and a restaurateur and tailor, both of whom were ex-directory. The Star Maker, recuperating from yet another operation and skin graft, was rumored to be watching in Casablanca, on a closed circuit via Telstar.

This was clearly the "in" set, Mortimer thought, looking around, pointedly unimpressed. London's celebrated swingers. Ordinarily he and Joyce would never have been included in such a charmed circle, but Ziggy Spicehandler who had directed this, the first Film of Fact, had written to the festival committee from Ibiza, and they had been sent tickets. This was uncharacteristically thoughtful of Ziggy, Mortimer thought, even middle-class, but only fair considering that he had lent him the money to buy his first handheld camera and had, well, starred in his first film. The usual home-movie stuff. Mortimer mowing the lawn, throwing Doug in the air, clowning at the barbecue, washing the car, clowning with Joyce, etc. etc.

Several years in the making, *Different* was, Mortimer had been led to believe, the most daring new-wave film yet to be made in England, but as a matter of fact it opened conventionally enough.

Fade in:

EXT. DAY. VATICAN CITY. ST. PETER'S SQUARE.

As the POPE is carried out among the faithful we see thousands upon thousands of them falling on their knees.

EXT. DAY. A FIELD

Working-class wheat bending obsequiously in the middle-class wind.

RESUME ST. PETER'S SQUARE. LONG SHOT.

In the far, far distance, a black-suited figure stands erect, the only one in thousands not on his knees.

ZOOM IN ON STANDING FIGURE.

A greasy, bearded Jew with a hooked nose looms over the faithful, chewing a sour pickle, the juice trickling down his chin.

Now faces were flashed on the screen. OSCAR WILDE. ISADORA DUNCAN. JOHN PROFUMO. HIMMLER. DYLAN. SAMMY DAVIS WEARING A SKULL CAP AND EATING GEFÜLLTE FISH. STEPHEN WARD. TROTSKY. MARILYN MONROE. RASPUTIN. DUKE OF WINDSOR. JUDAS. CATHERINE THE GREAT. LEE OSWALD. GIRODIAS. CASTRO. SENATOR JOSEPH McCARTHY. BERTRAND RUSSELL. JAMES DEAN.

Then, inexplicably, the film cut to:

CU WALL CAN OPENER

Hand opening an unlabeled can. As the can, ostensibly

empty, is inverted over a bowl, LAUGHTER pours out. Mad, zany laughter fills the screen.
SUPERIMPOSE laughter over a barefoot NEGRO BOY walking down a country road. Pursued by laughter he begins to run, run and run. But as the NEGRO BOY runs forward, the reactionary American landscape moves backward, leaving him in the same place.

As the swingers around Mortimer burst into applause, the screen went blank.

Silence. Nothing.

Finally Ziggy Spicehandler himself appeared on screen and wrote on a blackboard:

Presenting
A LIFE IN THE DAY OF JOHN JOHN JOHN

EXT. DAY. HAMPSTEAD GARDEN SUBURB. LONG TERRACE OF HOUSES.

Pan down a row of similar doors as they open and similar-looking husbands emerge, kiss similar-looking pretty wives goodbye and walk away whistling similar tunes to their similar cars . . . HOLD last door, last house.

EXT. DAY. HAMPSTEAD GARDEN SUBURB. LAST HOUSE. LAST GARDEN.

A DOG frolics on the grass.

ZOOM in on DOG'S EYE

Reflected in PUPIL is last door, last house, as

JOHN JOHN JOHN kisses his pretty wife.

The film then stayed with John John John as he went about his humdrum tasks in an office building that was clearly impersonal. Finally, his work done, John John John phoned to say he would be working late, and then off he drove.

SLOW DISSOLVE TO:

CU LOUIS XV CHANDELIER

MUSIC: Adam Faith sings "I Could Have Danced All Night."

TRACKING down to reveal

we are at a Drag Ball. PANNING over liberated, merry-making couples, finally

TRACKING IN on

CU JOHN JOHN JOHN

Dancing cheek to cheek with another MAN

FREEZE FRAME

COMMENTATOR (Voice Over)
Yes. John John John is different. He is a square peg in a round hole, an outsider, and in this square society . . . that's asking for trouble.

ENORMOUS CU JOHN JOHN JOHN

Rocking his head in his hands. Terror-struck. Sweaty.

The film then flash-cut to and fro from John John John to abusive, twisted faces shouting, "Fag!"
"Pouf!"
"Homo!"
"Queer!"
"Brown-noser!"
"Ladybird!"
"Sodomist!"

Mortimer sat cringing guiltily in his seat because the abusive, twisted faces were all nice clean-cut faces. Protestant faces. Handsome faces. Faces like his own.

ZOOMING IN ON JOHN JOHN JOHN'S EYEBALLS

Bloodshot. Trapped. As abusive voices quicken, become gibberish.

COMMENTATOR (Voice Over)
In a time of ticky-tacky conformists, there is a price to pay for being different.

EXT. DAY. DACHAU

The crematoria chimneys seen through a fog.

APPLAUDING HANDS

H-BOMB EXPLOSION

MORE APPLAUDING HANDS

NAPALM BOMBS FALLING ON VIET CONG

STILL MORE APPLAUDING HANDS

TWO MEN FRENCH-KISSING

CU POLICE WHISTLE

DISSOLVE TO:

INT. DAY. BLACKBOARD

A moving hand (ZIGGY SPICEHANDLER'S) writes:

"MAKE LOVE, NOT WAR."

After Make Love, Not War had been flashed at the audience in fourteen different languages, *Different* continued with still more episodes from homosexual life, alarming statistics, and examples of heterosexual atrocities. Then, suddenly, the scene shifted to Canada, Mortimer's native land, at the end of a National League hockey game at the Forum. A famous ALL-STAR DEFENSEMAN, one who was never without his helmet, was named first star of the game and skated round the rink to resounding cheers.

INT. FORUM. GANGWAY

As the PLAYERS make their way to the dressing room, rabid fans are still shouting the DEFENSEMAN'S name. FATHERS hold up their SONS to see him, GIRLS blow kisses.

INT. TEAM DRESSING ROOM

The ALL-STAR DEFENSEMAN slumps exhausted on the bench before his locker, drinking beer out of a can. As other players enter they slap him on the back or give him the thumbs-up sign.

ANOTHER ANGLE

ALL-STAR DEFENSEMAN kicks his locker open, revealing *Playboy* magazine pin-ups and a mirror on inside of door.

TRACK IN ON MOTTLED MIRROR

Broken, not of a piece, as is the case in the lives of some human beings.

MIRROR (POV ALL-STAR DEFENSEMAN)

His boisterous teammates light cigars, indulge in horseplay, spit, guzzle beer, pick their toes, scratch their groins . . . as they undress, removing pad after protective pad, strap after strap . . . gradually dispersing to showers.

ANOTHER ANGLE

ALL-STAR DEFENSEMAN now sits alone in dimly lit dressing room. Slowly, wearily, he rises and begins to get out of his pads and straps. As he sits down again, we are bound to notice that *one set of straps remains.*

ZOOM IN ON ALL-STAR DEFENSEMAN

They would appear to be brassiere straps!

ANOTHER ANGLE

As ALL-STAR DEFENSEMAN stands up and removes his helmet, we see a lovely sweep of golden hair, now inadequately concealed. This is the head of a YOUNG WOMAN in her prime.

PANNING down.

Her BODY, that of a fabulously vital animal, is one of those which clothes cover without hiding. The ALL-STAR DEFENSEMAN sighs . . . sighs again . . . her lovely body seemingly flooded with sudden longing . . .

LONG OVERHEAD SHOT. INT. FORUM. EMPTY.

Over the pure white ice steps the driven figure of the ALL-STAR DEFENSEMAN, her sensuality seemingly bound in a conformist's gray flannel suit and Presbyterian fedora. But is it?

SOUND: Soft strains of "Swan Lake."

And here (suddenly, miraculously), where only an hour ago the ALL-STAR DEFENSEMAN handed out murderous bodychecks, giving as good as she got . . . SHE now glides with balletic grace over the pure disinterested white ice, when:

FLASH-CUT TO LOUDSPEAKERS OVERHEAD

(in thick Protestant accents)

"DIFFERENT! DIFFERENT! DIFFERENT!"

RESUME LONG OVERHEAD SHOT

As ALL-STAR DEFENSEWOMAN flees.

Mortimer had hardly recovered from this shock when much of what he had seen earlier was now rerun at frantic speed, but intercut with a shot of a nice, well-adjusted man frolicking about his house and garden. So, from the beautiful but agonized young man mainlining heroin into his arm, the scene now shifted directly to the well-adjusted fellow mowing his lawn, singing. From the chimneys of Dachau the film cut to the same man pulling funny faces, crossing his eyes, as he washed his car. Next the camera zoomed in on two men french-kissing and zoomed out again on the well-adjusted man peeling a banana.

That well-adjusted man, that villain, was Mortimer.

Finally Mortimer was held in a frozen frame, winking, licking an ice cream. This frame was superimposed over an H-Bomb explosion, and scrawled in blood over Mortimer's face was one word:

WASP

As the audience rose to give *Different* a standing ovation, as all around Mortimer there were cries of "Bravo," he seized Joyce by the arm and fled the cinema, just making it outside before the lights came up. "That ungrateful son of a bitch," he said.

Joyce had to laugh. "Why, Mortimer, you amaze me. I thought Ziggy could do no wrong in your eyes."

"I don't want to talk about it." Joyce, he sensed, was pleased, enormously pleased. Mortimer took a deep breath and explained that had he been used so badly by anyone else but Ziggy, he would sue.

"But," Joyce said, delighted to finish what he had left unsaid, "as you have explained so many times before, this sort of dirty trick coming from Ziggy cannot be interpreted as an outrage. It –"

"Oh, shettup, will you?"

"It is but another of Ziggy's sardonic, but meaningful, jokes. Or is that not the case when the joke is so obviously directed at you?"

"I said I don't wish to discuss it."

"He's made a fool out of you."

"He has not. He most certainly has not. He has merely used my face for his own artistic purposes."

Ziggy had not even attended his own world premiere; he had had his name removed from the credits. In a statement distributed by students in the cinema foyer he explained that his film had been emasculated by the producers for commercial reasons. Some of his most finely wrought scenes had been excised from the finished print.

"All the same," a reporter asked, telephoning Ziggy the next morning, "don't you feel you're better off here than in Russia?"

"Not bloody likely," Ziggy said.

At least, the reporter went on to say, he was not being put on trial for his artistic beliefs. Unlike Andrei Sinyavsky and Yuli Daniel, he had not been sentenced to hard labor.

Mortimer's indignation was not mollified, but Joyce was more than somewhat pleased by Ziggy's astute retort to this typical bit of red-baiting.

"While I do not approve the recent sentences imposed on Sinyavsky and Daniel, it is a measure of just how seriously art and artists are taken in the Soviet Union."

Then Ziggy returned to the censorship question in the so-called freedom-loving West, where artists were considered jokers. He summed up the problem succinctly by saying so long as you couldn't pull your cock on TV his artistic freedom was impaired.

Eleven

MORTIMER LAY NUDE IN bed except for a scented black silken blindfold. Hands and heated tongue caressed him, rousing him, then a loving mouth came down on him, sucking, sucking. Gorgeous, he thought. Exquisite. Don't stop . . . Until a bass voice said, "You're yummy, baby. Real soul food," and he leaped up from the sheets, revealed to the world as a queer.

Different.

"No, no," he shouted, wakening.

Migod. Ziggy Spicehandler's film had left Mortimer with plenty of food for thought and with Joyce asleep beside him, he lit one cigarette off another. Am I a homosexual? he wondered. If, as Ziggy's film claimed, invoking the loftiest authorities, the type is *not* recognizable (limp wrists, fruity voice), then I can no longer be assured that I'm not one simply because I don't appear to be one. On the contrary. I may be one of the most noxious kind – the repressed homo. Even, he thought, my ostensible enjoyment of conjugal rights may be nothing more than overcompensation; a clever front.

What concerned Mortimer most deeply was that unlike Ziggy Spicehandler he had never had a homosexual trauma. Ziggy, possibly, was a bad example, if only because he would have had a homosexual experience, he had had all the advantages, famous public school, etc., etc. But Ziggy . . . Ziggy had tasted and rejected homosexual experience. Not Mortimer, however. Why, he thought, I find the very thought of a physical relationship with another man vomit-making. A dead giveaway, that.

Queers were an abomination to Mortimer. Waiting for Joyce in a pub unnerved him, especially West End pubs, which were thick with them. Naturally he always took a newspaper or magazine with him (if it was the *New Statesman*, he never had it open at the book pages) and made a point of glancing meaningfully at his watch again and again, so that no unattached man in the pub could possibly get the wrong idea and embarrass himself. Even so, single men had occasionally smiled at Mortimer or even tried to start up a conversation. Once, in the Yorkminster, a man standing beside him had said, the ploy pathetic, "Got a light, mate?"

"Now you stay away from me or I'll hit you," he said.

"What in the hell are you –"

"I'm a married man with a child," Mortimer protested, gulping down his drink and choosing to wait for Joyce outside.

And then, if Mortimer was going to be absolutely honest with himself about suppressed tendencies, he also had to own up to the barber bit. Mortimer was very, very choosy about barbers. He always had his hair cut in a shop where there were lots of them, so that he could select his chair circumspectly. Even so, he didn't trust himself to be shampooed any more and had to wash his hair at home now. What had happened was a couple of years back, at Simpson's, in Piccadilly, he had agreed to a shampoo with a scalp massage, was enjoying it hugely, until he discovered himself with an erection. Fortunately it wilted before the barber, a fatherly type, removed the protective sheet from him.

Mortimer had to admit to even another quasi-homosexual experience. When he and Joyce were still living in Canada, he used to make a habit of watching the hockey games on TV on Saturday nights, and thereafter, unaccountably, he always felt horny, which was not in itself suspect, but – but – but once in bed with Joyce, fiercely determined not to ejaculate too soon, he used to hold himself back, so to speak, by reliving the hockey game, eventually coming to his climax, eyes squeezed shut and mind closed to his thrusting, moaning partner, with the clear and exciting image of Gordie Howe bearing down on the nets to score; his ultimate joy synchronized – inadvertently, perhaps, with Joyce reaching her sexual summit, but consciously with Gordie Howe whipping the puck into the nets.

Am I a faggot? he thought.

Even the most bullish hetero, he'd read somewhere, had a smidgin of homosexuality in him. Yes, Yes, but how much was too much? Mortimer had devised a trial for himself, a trial he had never dared to take in waking life though he had had nightmares about it from time to time.

In his dream Mortimer lies nude except for a scented blindfold, he is tied to the sheets, roused by a probing tongue and adoring mouth, forced to submit to the test, rather like those endured by housewives on TV who are offered a fiver if they can tell Stork margarine from butter. Like them, he fails. He can't tell a man's mouth from a woman's. Furthermore, in his dreams he enjoyed being sucked immensely and was only disgusted after the fact if it turned out that it was a man who had been doing it.

And yet – and yet – something in Mortimer refused to accept that he was a homosexual. A more sensible inner voice assured him that it was a slight tendency, no more, a containable drive magnified in his mind, because he unconsciously appreciated how dull he was, a placid WASP with a regular job, and only craved depravity in the hope it would make him more interesting to such as Ziggy Spicehandler.

Or Polly Morgan? No, no; unlike every other man at Oriole

(and, according to rumor, at most other publishing houses) he was not out to make Polly. Not only, he thought, because I have no chance of success where everyone else has reportedly failed. I just don't give a shit about Polly Morgan, that's all.

Good old Ziggy, he thought, for he had already forgiven him. Unrepressed Ziggy, he thought, finally falling asleep.

Pale and weary, her gorgeous big blue eyes smarting, Polly Morgan emerged from the late movie at the Academy and hailed a taxi. Whew, she thought, for it was her fourth movie of the day. "Annabel's, please," she whispered.

Until he pulled up before the discothèque in Berkeley Square, the taxi driver, absorbed in a reverie of his own, didn't notice that his fare was no longer there. His taxi was empty. What the hell, he thought.

Entering her basement flat, Polly rested briefly with her back against the door. Her eyes twinkling, she sucked in an enormous breath, inflating her bosom, and then, quite suddenly, she kicked off her shoes. Arms outspread, Polly spun across the living room floor, skirt billowing high, as she floated toward her bedroom, finally tumbling to her bed, laughing secretively, joyously, as she wriggled free of her skirt and went to gaze out of the window.

A full moon stared back at Polly as she hummed the opening bars of the "Moonlight" Sonata. *He is looking at the same moon*, she thought.

Polly scooped up the red telephone. Holding it to her as she tumbled backward on the bed, her jet black hair simply ravishing against the white pillow, she began to sing into the receiver,

> Somebody loves me,
> I wonder who,
> Maybe, it's you.

Twelve

Mortimer leaped out of bed to collect the morning mail. There was a thick letter from his regiment, which he hastily tore up.

"Aren't you even going to read it?" Joyce asked.

"It's the anniversary of the battle. I know exactly what's in it," he said, putting a match to the pieces.

Hy Rosen put down his *Daily Express* and glared at Diana across the breakfast table.

"Where were you last night?" he demanded.

"For the last time, darling, I was at the movies. I –"

"If I ever catch you with another guy –"

"Another man? After your brutish demands, where would I find the energy?"

Heh-heh. Hy swept his arm across the breakfast table, sending boiled eggs, toast rack, milk jug and teapot crashing to the floor. "Into the bedroom with you," he said.

Diana swallowed a sob. Leaping up, hopeful yet incredulous, she asked, "First thing in the morning?"

"Come on." Hy clapped his hands together. "Mush!"

Dino Tomasso, taking breakfast at his desk at Oriole House, read in his morning newspaper that the postmen were going out on strike. They were asking for another fifteen shillings. Two dollars. Well, that wasn't exactly peanuts, maybe they would settle for half. Then Tomasso looked at the newspaper story again. No, no, they weren't asking for another two dollars an hour. Incredibly enough, what they seemed to want was two dollars more a week. Tomasso thrust the newspaper at Mortimer, the first to arrive for the morning conference. "Is this a misprint?" he asked.

"No."

Tears welled in Tomasso's eyes. "Oh, my God," he said, "how much are they paid now? Basic?"

"Oh, thirteen . . . fourteen pounds a week, possibly."

Tomasso thought his heart would break. O England, my England, where they haven't even got enough niggers to collect the garbage, but have to do it themselves.

The morning conference was dull, uneventful, until the efficiency experts from Frankfort appeared, bringing Tomasso a copy of the first title in the Our Living History series. The manuscript was delivered by Herr Dr. Manheim, two assistants in black leather coats, and Fräulein Ringler. "All right," Tomasso said, seemingly alarmed. "That's all for this morning, fellas."

Later, Mortimer sought Tomasso out. Like all the other old editorial hands, he naturally wanted the first two titles in the Our Living History series to fail, but now, with publication day approaching, his loyalty to Oriole and what it stood for overrode his distaste for Tomasso. Mortimer suggested that he would try to book a provincial speaking tour for the Labour politician. "Forget it, baby," Tomasso said. Mortimer offered to try to cajole one or another of the art cinemas into doing a season of the faded star's films. "Skip it," Tomasso said, chuckling.

"Look here, if my services have become redundant under the new order of things, all you have to do is let me know."

"But, Mort, you are being groomed to take over. Didn't you know that?"

"What?"

"The Star Maker especially asked to see your file. The Star Maker was enormously impressed."

"What, may I ask, did he find so impressive?"

Tomasso narrowed his eyes; he grinned smugly.

"Dino, I think the time has come for you and me to have a serious talk. There's a lot going on at Oriole that baffles me."

"Tomorrow maybe," Tomasso said, dismissing him.

Hy hadn't shown up for the morning conference and so immediately afterwards Mortimer went to his office. He wasn't there, either. Mortimer stopped Jennifer Mills in the hall. "Seen Hy?" he asked, concerned.

"No. But my guess would be the library. Or haven't you had the pleasure yet?"

"No."

"Our new librarian. Splendid body metabolism. And," she added acidly, "mammary glands that are absolutely super."

Mortimer didn't actually get to the library until six o'clock. The lights were out; it looked deserted. Mortimer was about to leave when a husky voice called out, "I'm in here."

The girl's voice came from behind the stacks, where the reference office was situated. The new librarian was the good-looking, elegantly dressed colored woman Mortimer had encountered in Lloyd's bank.

"Well, hullo there," she said, her smile teasing.

"Sorry to trouble you so late. I was looking . . . um . . . for Mr. Rosen."

"I don't recall a Mr. Rosen. Mind you, everyone else has been and gone. Now if you have a minute," she added, "I'll show you how I swing from stack to stack."

"Eh?"

"Or don't *you* think a colored librarian is a curiosity?"

"Certainly not. But, um, if people have been dropping in, perhaps it's because a girl as young and, ah, attractive as you are . . ."

"Well, thank you. My name is Rachel Coleman."

"I'm Griffin. Mortimer Griffin."

Rachel was wearing a green cashmere sweater and a white leather skirt, cut stylishly short. Mortimer coughed studiously loud so that if anybody happened to come into the library they would realize at once that he was making no attempt to conceal his presence. On the contrary. Then he helped Rachel into her coat. Her perfume was bewitching, but he dared not sniff emphatically lest she think he believed colored people had a peculiar smell.

Outside, they bumped into Jacob Shalinsky, of all people, carrying an enormous stack of his magazines. Touching his hat, Shalinsky grinned too knowingly for Mortimer's taste. "Good evening, Mr. Griffin . . . Ah, Miss Coleman."

"You know him?" Mortimer asked.

"Doesn't everybody in Soho know Jake? He's charming."

"He's an obnoxious bastard, that's what he is!"

"I had no idea," Rachel said, "that you were an anti-Semite."

She made that sound as if, to her delight, there was actually hair on his chest.

"Don't be absurd," Mortimer said, startled.

Which left them immediately outside The Eight Bells. "I suppose you wouldn't have time for a drink?" Mortimer asked, trapped.

"I'd love a drink."

Just my luck, Mortimer thought, all the regulars were there. The wide boys. Rapani the chemist from next door, Donnelly from the betting shop, Lawson, Gregory the headwaiter, Taylor, Wzcedak, and most of the others. As Mortimer entered with Rachel, who looked strikingly elegant, he sensed a wetting of lips all around him. Derek grinned lasciviously at him from behind the bar.

"I know," Rachel said, clapping her hands, "let's have champagne."

Mortimer looked amazed.

"A half bottle, then," she said.

Somewhere behind Mortimer's stinging red neck, Donnelly began to softly whistle "Roll Me Over in the Clover." Wzcedak caught Mortimer's eye in the bar mirror. He wiggled his ears at him. While Derek opened the champagne with unnecessary ceremony, Rachel went to make a phone call. Rapani the chemist was instantly by Mortimer's side. "Was getting worried about you, mate, you haven't been in my shop for a week now."

"The poor luv's beginning to feel his age," Taylor called out, bringing forth hoots.

Rapani, reeking of garlic, began to whisper in Mortimer's ear. "It was getting round to closing time and you hadn't been round for a whole bloody week –"

Wzcedak gave Mortimer the thumbs-up sign.

"– so I says to myself, use your loaf, Alex, and I brought the stuff with me."

Rapani slipped Mortimer the package. Fortunately just before Rachel returned to the table.

"We've met before," Mortimer said to Rachel, pouring the champagne. "At the bank, remember?"

"The bank," Rachel said, appalled. "Now I'm too late."

"Is there anything I can do?"

"Silly me. I meant to go, but it was my first day at Oriole – I haven't a penny."

"How much do you need?"

"Ten pounds. Would they cash a check for me here, do you think?"

"No, no, let me. I'll lend it to you."

"Oh, aren't you a sweetie," she said, waiting.

But Mortimer didn't hand over the money. Instead he drained his glass. "It's getting frightfully late. I'm taking a taxi. Going north. Can I drop you off?"

"If you're passing Baker Street –"

"Yes."

"But you must let me pay my share."

Once in the taxi, Rachel's skirt rode up. She made no attempt to adjust it. "Whee," she said, giggling. "One glass of champagne and I'm tiddly."

After last night's nightmares, his homosexual doubts, Mortimer was enthralled to discover a familiar warmth and upspringing in his genital area.

"You're not saying anything."

"Sorry," he said, handing Rachel the ten pounds.

"You wouldn't give it to me in the pub because of all those filthy-minded men there."

"That's not true," he lied.

"It is and it's very sensitive of you, Mortimer. Ooops, here we are."

As the taxi braked she was flung briefly against him. Hastily, he got out of his side of the taxi and raced round to open the door for her.

"This is where I live. I'm on the third floor." She gave him the phone number. "Will you remember it?"

"Yes, indeed."

Rachel kissed him shyly on the cheek and was off running, a flash of long brown legs.

Dining early at the Tiberio, Dino Tomasso couldn't eat his T-bone steak. He sent back his poire Hélène untouched. Finally, he summoned the waiter. "I want you to get me the Star Maker on the phone," he said, and he gave him the Las Vegas number.

"The Star Maker's not here," Miss Mott said. "The Star Maker is in the hospital again. *Thanks to you.*"

"Hey, hey there, that's no way to talk. Give me the hospital number."

It wasn't the usual place, but the clinic in Casablanca.

"Why there?" Tomasso asked.

"You ought to know, *you fool.*"

"Look, let's not play games. Just give me the number."

A half hour later Tomasso got the Star Maker on the line. Between sobs, he told the Star Maker about England's postmen. "Listen to me," he pleaded. "How many postmen can they have all together on this piddly little island? Let's us give them the two bucks."

"Impossible."

"Aw, come on, Star Maker. It wouldn't even make a dent."

"It's not the money. They would resent it. They'd call it dollar imperialism."

It's true, Tomasso thought.

"Star Maker, there's something else that's worrying me. It's Griffin."

"Not the boy with the marvy lymph system?"

"The same. Star Maker, he's asking a lot of questions. I don't like it."

"I'm glad you called, Dino," the Star Maker said.

"Is it good to hear my voice?"

"Ah ha."

"You have no heir, Star Maker. I'm your son."

The Star Maker laughed. "I'm just on my way to London. See you tomorrow, Dino."

Instantly, Tomasso put on his thick pebble glasses.

Thirteen

"OH, MY GOD," TOMASSO said, squinting behind his thick pebble glasses, "the Star Maker is here already."

Everybody at the morning conference got up to look. On the street below a motor cavalcade passed. Two men on motorcycles were followed by a Silver Cloud Rolls-Royce, an ambulance, a Brinks-type armored car, two Austin Princesses, a refrigeration truck and two more men on motorcycles.

The Star Maker, Mortimer knew, had come to London ostensibly to start production of a multimillion-dollar film which, as it happened, would feature Mortimer's longstanding favorite film Star. This is not to say that Mortimer was a tiresome film buff, addicted to camp: it was simply that this Star, the idol of Mortimer's adolescence, had amused him ever since. Of all the incomparably upright stars of a vintage era, Gable, Tyrone Power, Robert Taylor, John Wayne, Randolph Scott, Alan Ladd (decadence setting in, Mortimer felt, with Bogart and John Garfield), his heart, his boyish heart, had gone out to this Star alone. He was the most satisfyingly two-dimensional. Always, no matter what role he played, indisputably masculine, impossibly virtuous. Of all the Star Maker's dazzling discoveries, this Star – as far as Mortimer was concerned – was the greatest. And the most endearing.

"Do you think," Mortimer asked Tomasso, "I might be allowed to visit the studio one day and watch?"

"Absolutely against the rules. You know that."

Feeling foolish, Mortimer nevertheless asked, "Do you know him personally?"

"So?"

"What's he really like?"

"What are you, baby, a fan? You want me to get his autograph for you?"

"Well, I'm not *exactly* a fan," Mortimer said, hard put to conceal his rising anger, "it's just that this Star certainly has the emptiest face I've ever seen on screen."

"What are you getting at?" Tomasso demanded hotly.

"Take it easy, Dino. Calm down. Look at it this way. I was brought up on this Star. I've seen him return to Rome a conquering hero, advise Caesar, help Jesus carry the cross. I remember him sailing the Spanish Main, fighting three swordsmen with one hand behind his back, and winning the American Civil War almost single-handed. Why, he's won more gun fights than –"

"So *what?*"

"He's given me an inferiority complex. It would reassure me to visit the set and prove to myself that he's just as real as the rest of us."

"Are you out of your mind, Griffin?"

"Now look here –"

They were interrupted by a knock at the door. One of the black-suited motorcycle riders handed Tomasso an envelope, turned, and quit the office. Tomasso ripped open the envelope, read the letter inside, and collapsed in his chair.

"Is there anything wrong?" Mortimer asked.

Tomasso rocked his head in his hands. "Get out. Leave me alone."

The editors had only just dispersed when Tomasso, squinting behind his thick pebble glasses, wearing his coat, carrying his briefcase, emerged from his office. Two black-suited motorcycle riders waited in the hall, blocking his way. With them were Dr. Laughton and Gail. One of the riders was about to say something when Tomasso sighed, shook his head, and retreated into his office, Laughton and Gail following after. Gail, squealing with laughter, reached out and Tomasso handed her his glasses.

"You're a card, Dino," Laughton said, "You really are."

Agnes Laura Ryerson phoned.

"Do you remember," she asked, her voice quivering, "the very first birthday gift I ever gave you?"

Boys' Own Paper. " 'Fear God,' " Mortimer said warmly, " 'honor the crown, shoot straight and keep clean.' Does that answer your question?"

"I was just inquiring about the price of a subscription for Doug. It's stopped, Mortimer. There's to be no more *Boys' Own*. After eighty-eight years!"

Mortimer was flipping idly through the *Evening Standard* when he looked up from his desk to see Polly Morgan filling the door to his office, lips parted, tapping her teeth with her thumbnail. "May I come in?" she asked.

"Certainly."

The *Standard* was opened at a full-page ad for *The Longest Day*, now at popular prices.

"Ken Annakin," Polly said, indicating the ad, "Andrew Marton, Bernard Wicki. Zanuck. 20th. 1962. Grossed 15,100,000 so far."

"What's that?"

"I'll only take a second of your time," Polly said, sitting down.

Polly wore a black leather Dutch boy's cap and a tight sweater, right half white, left half blue: one high and lovely breast circumscribed by a yellow bolt, the other by a green one, and Mortimer aching to do nothing so much as tighten them.

"Just wanted to say that . . . like we're having a scene on Saturday night. At Timothy's pad."

"Oh," Mortimer said, heart leaping.

"It should be jolly good fun. Do you want to come?"

Unfortunately Mortimer realized he was only being invited because he was such a good friend of Ziggy Spicehandler's – a relationship which confounded the hipsters among his acquaintances.

"Well, thanks. Um, I'll give it some thought."

Then Mortimer made his gaffe. Error in etiquette. As Polly rose from her chair he shot round without thinking to open the office door for her. Polly, to her credit, did not laugh, but Mortimer was bloody embarrassed and he knew right then he would not go to the party because he was bound to do the wrong thing. Make a fool of himself. Though he'd remember to say "cunt" often, saying it he'd betray self-consciousness.

"You're shy," Polly said.

"Am I?"

"I know you like a book, Mortimer Griffin."

He laughed lamely.

"You're going to stop fighting me," Polly said, stepping closer to him, "aren't you?"

Avoiding The Eight Bells, Mortimer took Polly to a pub on Mount Street for lunch.

"This will be our special place now," she said, crinkling her nose. "Won't it?"

Mortimer agreed emphatically.

"I want to understand you. Who you are. What you are."

But when Mortimer returned from the bar with a second round of drinks it was to discover that Polly was no longer at their table. She hadn't left the pub, however. Polly sat at another table on which there were at least a dozen empty glasses and an overflowing ashtray. "I'm going to be ill," she said. "You must hate me."

"No, no. But I don't understand –"

"Please take me home."

Mortimer dashed outside, where he soon found a taxi, but when he returned to fetch Polly it was too late: she had already vanished.

Polly did not return to Oriole House in time to watch the Star Maker being interviewed on TV.

Getting the Star Maker to appear on TV was no mere matter of fees or flattery or agreeing to questions or an appropriately obsequious interviewer. It was much more complicated than that. Wherever the ageless, undying Star Maker went, an emergency medical unit, unrivaled for excellence, had to be accommodated. The kidney-cleansing technicians had first to check the power plugs and establish themselves with batteries in the event of a power failure. The cardiologists and their awkward pump, complete with artificial valves and mechanical heart, had to be similarly catered to. So did the blood plasma boys and nurses. The Star Maker's irreplaceable urinologist had to be satisfied, so did the sexologist, a Danish fusspot, newly arrived, and looked down upon as kinky by the rest of the unit. Then one of the guards had to establish a clear run to the refrigeration truck and interconnecting operating ambulance that always waited on the boil within five minutes of the Star Maker, the spare-parts men and their priest ready for any sacrifice in the Austin Princess immediately behind.

It was perhaps a testimony to the much-abused Star Maker's essential affability that everybody in the unit except the Danish sexologist and, understandably, the spare-parts men who had to be constantly renewed, had been with the Star Maker for years. They were old buddies, equipped to meet any crisis, but relaxed, given to private jokes and high-spirited card games.

The Star Maker was interviewed in his own specially designed suite at the film studios, seated in a wheelchair in the shadows, the patch over the left eye just visible.

The patch, naturally, led to instant speculation among reporters, especially those from financial newspapers, for it added pungency to recent rumors that the ageless, undying Star Maker was afflicted with cataracts. Ageless, but possibly, just possibly, not undying after all. If cataracts were only a rumor, cancer was all but established fact. The Star Maker spoke in wheezing, metallic tones, the voice coming through a tube rumored to be platinum.

All the editors at Oriole Press, including Mortimer, assembled in Dino Tomasso's office to watch the interview.

"Could you tell us," the interviewer finally asked, "why you are called the Star Maker?"

As Mortimer watched, an incredible thing happened. The Star Maker actually laughed. The flesh round the mouth creased and the good eye began to water, spilling over with malevolence, before the face retreated into the shadows again. An eerie scratchy noise rose from the mouth.

"No," Tomasso cried, rushing up to the TV screen. "No, Star Maker. No."

The Star Maker's smile ebbed slowly. "I should have thought it obvious, son."

"But aren't you being somewhat vain? Clearly you don't make stars, only God –"

Tomasso began to mutter to himself; he seemed to be praying.

"You may have discovered and promoted stars," the interviewer said, "but –"

"That's all I've ever done," the Star Maker said, hand held over the heart, "that and no more."

The television image faded and Oriole's editors drifted out of Tomasso's office one by one. Only Mortimer stayed behind, curious to see Tomasso so troubled.

"He's so rich," Mortimer said idly, "and yet, well, he hasn't even got a son."

"I am his son. I've got it on paper. 'You are my son, Dino.' "

"Has he never married, then?"

"The Star Maker? How could he, Griffin? There isn't a person in the world worthy of his love."

"Did the Star Maker actually say that?"

"Something like that." Tears welled in Dino Tomasso's eyes. "I am his son. That's the Star Maker's promise to me. Now, if you don't mind, there are some things I must clear up before . . ."

"Before what?"

"The Star Maker expects every man to do his duty. That will be all, Griffin."

On the tarmac opposite Sound Stage D, where the Star Maker's emergency medical unit was parked, laughter spurted from within the ambulance-cum-operating theater. Drunken laughter. The doors whacked open and a group of doctors and nurses tottered out, gaily chanting, "*We want a kidney. We want a kidney.*"

Led by Laughton and Gail, they descended hand in hand on the Austin Princess, where the spare-parts people sat, cowering. One of the spare-parts men began to sob. As he was armless himself, his companion, a thoughtful fellow, held a Kleenex to his nose.

"*We were only kidding,*" the doctors and nurses now chanted. "*We were only kidding.*"

Within the Star Maker's suite, Miss Mott handed the Star Maker the phone. "It's Tomasso. He's in a very excited state."

"I shouldn't wonder."

Tomasso told the Star Maker everything Mortimer had said about the Star. He repeated all the offensive remarks.

"Oh, really, Dino, you've become such a worrier. He's an intellectual. It's typical sour grapes."

Tomasso wasn't convinced.

"Very well, then, keep an eye on him. But you're too touchy, Dino. That's a fault in you."

Fourteen

AT MORTIMER'S NEXT "Reading for Pleasure" lecture, on Monday night, Jacob Shalinsky was not alone. He sat with a tiny pinched man with rimless glasses. Throughout Mortimer's lecture the tiny pinched man took notes; he and Shalinsky whispered together, Shalinsky nodding approvingly more than once. Afterwards, by prearrangement, Mortimer grudgingly sought Shalinsky out at the corner pub. He handed Shalinsky his twelve-hundred-word article on Chagall, titled – rather catchily, he thought – "The Myopic Mystic," and ordered drinks for the two of them. Shalinsky read Mortimer's piece at once, pondering it unsmilingly. Finally he folded it neatly in four, pocketing it without comment.

"Is there anything the matter?" Mortimer asked.

"Cracking good stuff, *magnifique*, as an intellectual exercise, but –"

"You don't have to print it if you don't want to."

"Did I say I wouldn't print it? Not bloody likely . . . but, if you'll allow me to finish, I had hoped it would be a little more from the soul. Take the title, for instance. The Myopic Mystic," he said with obvious distaste. "Easy alliteration. Clever. Too clever by half, Mr. Griffin. No heart. I'll tell you a good title. I. M. Sinclair wrote an appreciation of Isador Zangwill on the anniversary of his death and you know what he called it? 'I Continually Worship Those Who Are Truly Great.' But does Sinclair have your insights into the human psyche? No. This is a smashing article, Mr. Griffin. I wouldn't change a word. Not for the world."

Just then Mortimer's jacket was given a fierce tug from behind. He whirled around to confront the tiny pinched man with rimless glasses.

"What," the man snapped, "do you think of the work of J. Genet? Answer me that."

"Well, I –"

"Ordure. Compulsive offal pure and simple. You've read the so-called novels of K. Amis?"

"I'm afraid we haven't been introduced."

"I am I. M. Sinclair. Does that mean anything to you?"

"Mr. Shalinsky has mentioned your name to me. You're a doctor, I believe."

"Like Chekhov."

"Oh. Oh, I see."

"I'm the only honest critic in Golders Green. Go ahead, laugh. *I* care." Then, as though he were composing on the spot, Sinclair continued, "I am an old man . . . an old man in a dry month . . . waiting for rain."

Ignoring Mortimer's protests, Shalinsky ordered another round of drinks. "I told I.M. about your Kafka lecture and he insisted on coming along tonight."

"Oh. Oh, I see."

"It seems to be your contention, Griffin," Sinclair said, "and you may correct me if I'm wrong, that Kafka's strict Jewish upbringing had a crippling effect on the man –"

"A Jewish education," Shalinsky interrupted solemnly, "never harmed anybody."

"Would you say, then, this is also true of E. Hemingway, who had a strict Catholic upbringing?"

"Um, no."

"Then," I. M. Sinclair continued, "are you aware, Griffin, that your insinuation, that your very approach to the Kafka enigma –"

"Now look here, Doctor –"

"– may be motivated by the perfidy of anti-Semitism, no matter how artfully intellectualized? And that, therefore, most of your opinions on the subject, apart from being derivative, are also intellectually disreputable?"

Shalinsky stepped between the two men. "I brought you," he said to Mortimer, "some back issues of *Jewish Thought*. A representative selection."

Flipping through the magazines, Mortimer was astonished to find, side by side with the outlandish, contributions by major Jewish writers and by international figures on the Jewish question. "It's all very impressive," he said.

"The hammer looms over us. *Jewish Thought* is on the verge of bankruptcy, Griffin. Unless there is a miracle our next issue – the Annual Arts & Artists number – may very well be our last to appear."

"You said that last year, Jake. And the year before."

"But this year I'm in deadly earnest. Advertising no longer brings in the revenue it used to and printing costs are constantly on the rise. Mr. Rothstein –" Shalinsky hesitated, he turned to Mortimer. "Rothstein's Clothing; he's our angel . . . is growing weary of pouring hard-earned money –"

"Tax deductible."

"– into a stagnant venture. His sons, both of them philistines, are against our magazine. Now I happen to believe, Griffin, that the uses of *Jewish Thought* cannot be measured in shillings and pence. It has to do with our psyche, and it must not perish in this shallow I'm-all-right-Jack society."

"*Gut gezagt.* Agreed. But we're an isolated group – Golders Green cares only about money and status and the young."

I. M. Sinclair asked, turning fiercely on Mortimer, "Are they worried our culture might perish? No. Being gear, that's what they worry about."

"Possibly," Mortimer began, "they are no different –"

"I will speak plainly," I. M. Sinclair said. "What motivates the big Jewish givers in this country?"

"Well, I –"

"What motivates them," Sinclair continued, "is the hope of a knighthood or at least an M.B.E."

"Let's face it," Shalinsky said, "there are no titles in *Yiddishkeit*."

"The Queen cares our culture may perish? She married a German."

"To put the problem more concretely," Shalinsky said mournfully, "if we could only reach a circulation of two thousand – and our present circulation is less than half that – Mr. Rothstein has promised to support us for another year at least."

"Mr. Shalinsky," Mortimer said, "I'd like to take out a subscription to *Jewish Thought*. I'll send you a check tomorrow. Maybe I can even interest some of my friends."

"If you can, I won't forget the commission."

"*Thanks*. And now I really must go."

"Won't you stay and have another drink with us?"

"Sorry, but my wife's waiting up for me."

Shalinsky walked to the pub door with Mortimer. "And now," he said, "I must thank you once more for your essay. I am honored to print you, Griffin. *Merci mille fois*."

"It's you I ought to thank. I, um, enjoyed speaking with you and Dr. Sinclair immensely."

"I knew it. You see," Shalinsky said, squeezing his elbow, "it's good to be with your own sometimes."

Mortimer broke rudely free of him. "Just what do you mean by that?"

Shalinsky shrugged; he looked at the floor.

"Shalinsky, will you please get it through your head that I'm not Jewish."

"But Griffin, Griffin, darling boy, what greater pleasure can there be than being a Jew?"

"Good night, Shalinsky."

Fifteen

"NOW COME ON, DOUG. Enough is enough," she called out.

But he absolutely refused to get out of the bath. "Can't I play just a little bit longer?" he pleaded.

The water, Joyce saw, was up to his chin. Plastic boats floated in the tub. So did a beach ball.

"Have you any idea why you want to stay longer in the tub –"

"Because it's jolly good fun."

"*– with the water up to your chin?*"

"Because it's jolly good fun."

"No. That's only the superficial reason. The real reason is because it makes you feel secure. Like," Joyce said, puffing out her stomach, "you were still floating in the waters inside me."

Doug's hand flashed out to pull the plug.

"Don't twitch."

"I'm not twitching."

"If you remember the picture book I showed you –"

"Y-y-y-es I do! Honestly!"

"The bag you floated in is called the membrane and you fed off a placenta." Suddenly Joyce bared her teeth. "See?"

"What?" he asked, shivering.

"The fillings. The decay."

"Yes."

"While you were growing inside me, you took the best part of my calcium."

"I'm sorry."

"You mustn't be. It's a natural thing. Neither should you apologize for feeling very, very safe in deep warm water. Many grown men feel the same way."

"Daddy too?"

"Daddy more than many. It's called a retreat to Mother's womb."

"I see," Doug said, drying himself.

"You're so lucky, Doug. I was brought up on lies, you know. My father – and he was a doctor, you know – told me that the stork had brought me."

Doug managed a deprecating laugh.

"He never told me I came out of my mother's vagina, just like you came out of mine. I had to learn about orgasms all by myself."

"He told you lots of lies, didn't he?"

"Too many," she said, following him into his bedroom.

"Remember the lie about Christmas?"

"Which one?"

"How he used to buy you smashing presents with money taken from poor patients and then pretend that Santa Claus had come down the chimney with them? How you and your brothers used to crawl out of bed at dawn to see what Santa had brought . . . and your father would be sitting there, waiting for you, drinking White Russian vodka and smoking non-union cigarettes?"

"Yes."

"Could you tell me that lie tonight? With all the details?"

"Not again. We're going to read another chapter from our book instead."

The bedtime book was *Hiroshima*. An illustrated edition. They had already finished reading Hilberg's *The Destruction of the European Jews.* Both volumes had become mandatory once Joyce had discovered that Doug had a cowboy gun hidden under his pillow. She wanted him to understand clearly where gunplay led to.

"Well now," Joyce said, shutting the book at last, "that's enough for tonight. Good night, Doug."

"Where's Daddy?"

"Lecturing. He'll be home late. Good night."

"Good night, Mother."

Two hours later Joyce was startled to see Doug standing at the door of her bedroom. He was red-eyed and shivering.

"What is it now?" Joyce asked.

"I had a scary dream."

Joyce slipped into her dressing gown, got out of bed, and turned off the television. Meanwhile, Doug slid into her bed.

"And what, may I ask, do you think you're doing?"

"Could I just lie here with you for a minute?" Doug asked, his teeth chattering.

"Only if you fully face up to why you want to lie in bed with me."

"It's because I'm scared, Mother."

"Balls. It's because you desire to make physical love to me. You wish to supplant your father."

"I do not!"

"But it's perfectly natural, Doug. All sons are secretly in love with their mothers. I just want you to be truthful with me, as I am with you. Now, why do you want to get into bed with me . . . when your father's out?"

Doug looked at the floor.

"A straight question deserves a straight answer, don't you think?"

"Yes, Mother."

"Well, then?"

"I think," Doug said, leaping off the bed as soon as she sat down beside him, "I'll go back to my own room now."

"That's being a very mature boy, Doug. I'm proud of you."

"Why?"

"Because this way you will suffer no psychological damage. When you're a grown-up you'll never need an analyst. Like I did. Good night, Doug."

"Good night, Mother."

Doug had only just gone back to his room when Mortimer came in.

"Well, well," Joyce said snidely, "Malcolm Muggeridge returns."

"What's eating you?"

"Doug's had another nightmare. Mortimer, why must they show those dreadful canned American TV shows here? The violence does children irreparable harm, I think."

Mortimer failed to respond.

"How did the lecture go tonight?" she asked.

"Skip it."

"What's wrong?"

"I don't want to talk about it, that's all."

"You've left a cigarette burning on the bureau."

"Oh, for Christ's sake! It would be nice not to have all my filthy little habits pointed out to me for once. I know there's a cigarette burning on the bureau."

Retreating into the bathroom, Mortimer closed the door softly behind him. He lit another cigarette and lingered in the tub. The water up to his chin.

"What on earth are you doing in there?" Joyce called out.

"Next time you use my razor on your blessed armpits, *darling*, I'll thank you to wash it and replace the blade."

"Now who's pointing out whose filthy habits?"

Mortimer didn't like mirrors. He made a point of never sitting opposite one in a restaurant, but tonight he had an urgent reason for studying his face. His conventionally handsome, suburban face.

"Mortimer!"

Mortimer. Morty. Mort. "Joyce," he said, coming out of the bathroom, "would you say I had a – a" – he almost said "Jewy," but bit it back – "a Jewish face?"

Joyce laughed.

"I'm serious."

"And what if you had? Would it be so awful?"

"Will you please just answer my question."

"As far as I'm concerned there's no such thing as a Jewish face."

"Let me put it to you this way, then. If there was such a thing as a Jewish –"

"There are no ifs about it."

"Why do you assume it is necessarily pejorative?"

"What?"

"A Jewish –"

"There is no –"

"There is no such thing as a Jewish face. Okay, okay."

"Now, will you please explain why you are in such a state?"

Mortimer told her about his meeting with Shalinsky at the pub.

"If you want my opinion," she said, "you wouldn't mind his notion in the least if you weren't a sublimated anti-Semite."

"Thank you," he said, switching off the light, "and good night."

But he was far too disturbed to sleep.

"I've been thinking, darling," Joyce said, "if you were Jewish –"

"*What?*"

"I mean if you've got Jewish blood, I'd love you just as –"

"Of all the stupid nonsense. What do you mean *if* I'm Jewish? You've met my parents, haven't you?"

"All I'm saying is that if –"

"All right. I confess. My father's real name is Granofsky. He's a goddamned defrocked rabbi. Not only that, you know, but my mother's really a coon. She –"

"Don't you dare use that word."

"Look, for the tenth time. If I had Jewish blood I wouldn't try to conceal it. Whatever made you think . . ."

"Well, you know."

"I told you long ago that was done for hygienic reasons. My mother insisted on it. Since I was only about two weeks old at the time, I wasn't consulted."

"Okay, I just wanted you to know where I would stand if –"

"Let's go to sleep. I've had enough for one day."

Still, sleep wouldn't come. Stealthily, careful not to wake Joyce, Mortimer retreated to the living room, poured himself a drink, and leaned back in his favorite easy chair.

Herzog sat on the coffee table. *Herzog*, which he had tried to read but which made him feel like an intruder, a Gentile peeper. And stuffy as well. Yes, yes, Mortimer thought, a good credit risk, that's me. Loyal. Hardworking. Honest. Liberal. The well-dressed fellow on the bench in *Zoo Story*. The virtues I was raised to believe in have become pernicious. Contemporary writing, he thought, is clawing at my balls, making me repugnant to myself. An eyesore. "Protestant," he said aloud. "White Anglo-Saxon Protestant filth, that's what you are."

Ugly. Ziggy Spicehandler, to whom Mortimer owed so much, once told him about a Korean folk singer who said that during World War II, when the Japanese had occupied Korea, they had shown films they had taken of American POW's. Nobody in the village, the Korean said, had ever seen a white man in the flesh and they could not believe what they saw in the film. "They thought the Japs were putting them on. They couldn't dig," Ziggy said, "that any cat could be born so ugly. You know, the white skin with the purple veins showing right through. The big feet. *Eyelids.* The elders in the village thought the film was Japanese propaganda. Nobody could be that ugly."

Ugly.

Mortimer's ugliness, first revealed to him by Ziggy Spicehandler, had come home most directly the night he had gone to see the first Cassius Clay–Henry Cooper fight. How justified Clay had been to say, "I'm the most beautiful." The glossy ebony body. The sensual face. The graceful manner of moving. All this pitted against – against, Mortimer thought, one of ours. Gray, doughy, fart-filled Henry Cooper. A body that was the lumpy sum of sausages and mash. Cooper absorbed one punch and instantly the flesh bruised, flooding red. Cooper's flesh, like Mortimer's, was Protestant: not made for the sun. On the beach it burns and blisters and peels.

Murder him, Mortimer had thought – identifying, to his astonishment, with Clay – destroy the ugly pink blob. Then the eye split, gushing hot thick blood, and Clay, ever fastidious, stepped back, appalled.

No more cigarettes. Mortimer went off in search of his jacket, dipped into a pocket, and came up with a small package. Rapani's. God damn it. Mortimer found his keys, unlocked the hall cupboard, and –

"Mortimer?"

– stowed away the package, but didn't have time to lock the cupboard again.

Joyce found him back in the easy chair, eyes shut. "Mortimer?"

"Mn?"

"There's a lit cigarette in your hand. You'll burn a hole in the chair."

"Oh."

"What are you doing in here anyway?"

"Thinking."

Joyce waited.

"Would you allow," he asked, "that there was such a thing as a *Negro* face?"

"Some of your jokes are in the worst possible taste."

"Yes, I know. I happen to be cursed with what Hy calls a Gentile sense of humor."

"Let's go to sleep."

"Sure." Mortimer let Joyce lead the way back to the bedroom, swinging the offending cupboard door shut with a kick. It locked.

Sixteen

IT HAD BEEN INSTIGATED by the wide boys at The Eight Bells, Mortimer's office local – no, no, that's not fair – the real reason behind the locked cupboard was Mortimer's increasingly obsessive fear that he didn't have a big one.

At last stocktaking, the embarrassing hoard in Mortimer's locked cupboard had included more than a dozen tubes of vaginal jelly, a number of diaphragms (running from small to super large), a plentiful supply of Durex prophylactics and contraceptive pills, and bottle upon bottle of varied and perfidious sexual stimulants and erection-promising powders and herbs. The jelly wouldn't burn with the autumn leaves and Mortimer was too ashamed to leave unused tubes for the dustmen. Oxfam, possibly, would have accepted the prophylactics, but when he had once been intrepid enough to try them with a phone call, he was passed from one party to another until a severe voice, unmistakably Pakistani, had asked him for his name and phone number, which he had refused. Even so, Mortimer might have mailed a parcel to Oxfam anonymously, if he hadn't feared that Scotland Yard, which had its methods, might trace the parcel to him. From time to time, he lightened his stock of pills, dissolving some in the toilet bowl. Other days, his pockets bulging with packets of Durex, he'd gone to Hampstead Heath, strewing

French letters here, there and everywhere. Still, the stuff tended to accumulate.

A sex maniac's hoard, he thought, and what about the cost? The same money invested in National Development Bonds or Scot-Bits rather than Rapani's astonishing variety of aphrodisiacs – but that's neither here nor there. The truth was Mortimer had been driven to stockpiling the stuff because of his mounting anxieties about the size of his thingee. Yes, yes, he knew size wasn't everything. Owing to vasocongestion, that is to say, swelling of the veins, it had been scientifically proved that a thin and puny one was bound to enlarge to a relatively greater degree than a whopping one. *All the same, mate, it's still smaller, isn't it?*

Mortimer hadn't been born with this feeling of inadequacy. Neither had it bothered him much in adolescence. If he ever overcame his shyness sufficiently in the showers after a basketball game to glance at somebody else's rod, it never struck him as being outlandishly bigger than his. On the other hand, all men suffered shrinkage in the showers and so that may have been a faulty proving ground.

Digging even deeper into his Caribou, Ontario, boyhood, to Motke Shapiro, the only Jewish boy at Caribou High, he could remember him saying, "Do you know why Queen Elizabeth is disappointed in George VI?"

"No. Why?"

"Because she's found out not every ruler has twelve inches."

Twelve. Did anybody actually have twelve inches, he thought, or, conversely, did everybody but me –?

Motke Shapiro was the only boy Mortimer remembered as being singularly well-endowed and consequently, perhaps, a show-off. He was forever entreating the other boys to join him in a communal pee. "See this," he'd say, shaking it at them. "This is a Jew's harmonica."

Or,

"Tell your sisters what you saw here. And if they don't believe it," he'd add, zipping up, "well, here I am, eh, guys?"

Right there, Mortimer felt, was planted the corrupting seed of his discontent, his suspicion that minority-group pricks (Jewish, Negro) were aggressively thicker and longer than WASP ones. And yet – and yet – though he had never cohabited with a colored girl, Mona Capelovitch, the one Jewess he'd had, never made denigrating remarks about him. His fear of derisory size, lying in wait in his unconscious for years, was released by literary experience. Book learning from Baldwin, Mailer, LeRoi Jones.

It seemed to be the philosophical contention of these talented, decidedly outspoken writers and thinkers, however much they differed in style and argument, that the average male Negro had a bigger cock and more thrust power than the average WASP. Furthermore this Holy Grail of a Negro cock was lusted after, consciously or unconsciously, by white women and created fear and trembling among white men, which was why Negroes were not wanted in white neighborhoods. Something else. While it offended Baldwin, Jones, and other Negroes no end to be told they were naturally musical or athletic, they were willing to allow that they did share one racial characteristic: big pricks.

Well, maybe yes, maybe no, Mortimer thought, but couldn't they be more scientific about it? Take James Baldwin, for instance. Clever dick that he undoubtedly is, how does he know Negro cocks are bigger than white ones? It isn't the sort of thing one can comparison-shop, is it, and in the natural order of things a guy simply doesn't get the opportunity to measure one against the other. How in the world would he or, come to think of it, Mailer or LeRoi Jones ever get to see so many pricks, regardless of race, color or creed? It's not as if they were the sort to hang around public conveniences, spying. Mortimer didn't get it. His problem was he *suspected* he was small, but he couldn't tell for certain.

He had seen other cocks, bigger cocks, on statues, yes, but this could have been a case of art improving on life. Like Andy Warhol making his Campbell's soup tins larger than they were in the supermarkets. At the same time, Mortimer had to allow that these writers were more gifted and intelligent than he was and so they must know whereof they spoke. Possibly the knowledge was intuitive. An insight. Like Mailer's discovery that cancer in America was caused by Protestants. Protestants like me, he thought.

Goddamn it, Mortimer thought, he didn't even know how many inches Hy, his best friend, had, and it wasn't the sort of thing he'd ask him. Or Diana.

Which brought him round to thinking about Joyce.

Not to brag, Mortimer would still say he satisfied her. Naturally there were times when he ejaculated too quickly and other occasions when he botched it through drunkenness, but, on balance, he'd hazard Joyce was not a frustrated wife. And yet – and yet – she might have no enormous need for sex or, conversely, her desires might be profligate but unfulfilled. Is our marital life full, Mortimer thought, or is it niggardly? Here again he had to confess to inexperience; he simply didn't know what other couples said or did in bed. Once more he was indebted to Ziggy and literary experience, both of which made him fear inadequacy, a lack of imagination.

Ziggy and the chicks: Migod, he certainly never failed for them, did he? Fondly, warmly, Mortimer recalled his first meeting with Ziggy, shortly after the war, in the Red Lion pub in Soho, where Ziggy, his first adolescent poems out in *New Writing*, was a legend. No sooner had Mortimer been introduced than Ziggy invited him to join his group. My round, Ziggy insisted, doubles for everyone, discovering too late that he had forgotten his bloody wallet at home. Mortimer happily paid for the drinks and several rounds later he was flattered to be asked to continue with Ziggy and his bunch to a party in a squalid basement in Camden Town. Those were the days, Mortimer reflected, remembering how he literally bumped into Ziggy feeling up the prettiest girl at the party in a dark damp corner. The girl was especially exciting to him, Ziggy explained later, because she was pregnant by his best friend.

Embarrassed, groping for any excuse to retreat, Mortimer noticed the girl's pint-sized beer mug was only half full. "What are you drinking?" he asked, reaching for the glass.

"His," the girl replied, her eyes seething.

Mortimer hadn't grasped the full import of what she meant (after all, British beer was notoriously flat) until Ziggy began to chortle at his discomfort.

"But – but – couldn't that be, well *unhealthy?*"

"If you really want to know," the girl said, "I've never felt so close to him before. Now bugger off, please."

Mortimer had melted away gratefully, suppressing nausea. But come noon the following day he was seeking out Ziggy at the Red Lion.

"You want her," Ziggy said, willing to arrange it for a fiver.

"No!"

"Quite right. She's thoroughly middle-class, actually. What I mean is she goes with dogs, but stops at great Danes."

Possibly, Mortimer thought, if our sex life is conformist, it's not completely my fault. Joyce could be partially to blame. Not once, flooded with passion, had she ever bit his ear to make it bleed. Or called out to him, "Fuck me good, Daddy-o!" Why? Did he inhibit her? Would she make such licentious requests of other partners? He didn't know. Once, only once, inspired by a novel he had just finished before they got into bed, had he walloped her on the buttocks, as they were enjoined in the most banal of love positions. There they were, he recalled, he thinking of Gordie Howe bearing down on the nets, she thinking of God knows what, when he had suddenly reared back and landed her an open-handed belt on the buttocks, but instead of releasing the animal needs in Joyce, it made her cry. She cried and cried, throwing him over and calling him names, not bracingly obscene, but clinical.

Bitch. She may be nonconformist-minded, he thought vengefully, but she undoubtedly had an establishment cunt.

Mortimer's shrinking confidence, his wilting prick, assailed by minority-group litterateurs and conjugal doubts, had been further abused in contacts with the hoi polloi. Two topics of conversation were all-pervasive at The Eight Bells: geegees and sex. Mortimer did not play the horses and to judge by the early and prejudiced reception he got from Donnelly, Rapani, Gregory, Taylor and Wzcedak, you'd think he had no sex life either; if only because he was undeniably middle-class, his manner reticent, his dress neat. Once, in the early days, Mortimer had entered a pub to find the men linked round Rapani, who was reading aloud from a paperback that had just been published:

> He reached down with both hands and grabbed the front of her dress. The fabric came away with a rasping, tearing sound. He put his hands inside her brassiere and pulled her breasts up and out. She stared at him, a fear growing deep in her eyes as once more he stood over her. Slowly he lowered himself onto her breasts until he was sitting facing her.
>
> He looked down at her and laughed. "Now, tell me. Examine it carefully. See, am I not the biggest man you ever saw?"
>
> Despite his weight she managed to nod.

Donnelly clacked his tongue approvingly.

"Not bad," Wzcedak said.

Gregory pulled his lower lip. "It's Harold Robbins. I recognize the style. With that man, the words leap off the page."

"Wait, wait," Rapani said, turning to another page. "Here's something even better."

"You're an animal."

Dax grinned. "It isn't that. What do you expect when you're standing there naked?"

She stared at him for a moment, then squashed her cigarette in a plate and dropped to her knees beside the bed. Tenderly she touched him. "*Quelle armure magnifique*," she whispered. "So quick, so strong. Already he is too large for both my hands to hold."

She –

"Not bloody likely," Taylor said, aggrieved.

"You think Rapani's making it up?" Gregory asked.

Taylor stared coldly at Rapani over the rim of his beer glass.

"But he couldn't. Rapani's no writer," Wzcedak said.

"Oh, for Christ's sake. Finish the passage."

"It says here, she says, quote: 'Already he is too large for both my hands to hold.'"

She buried her face against him. He felt the warmth of the tiny edges of her tongue tingling his flesh. He crushed her head against him.

"Unquote." Rapani looked up to notice for the first time that Mortimer was standing on the edge of the group. "Oh," he said.

Embarrassed, Mortimer raised his glass to Rapani. Rapani slammed the paperback shut. "Good evening, Mr. Griffin," he said.

It had been like that every time. Simply because Mortimer was always courteous and occasionally carried a furled umbrella, his entry into the pub, like a prissy schoolmaster's into an unruly classroom, had been inhibiting to the regulars. If, for instance, Gregory was relating one of his endless run of dirty stories or Wzcedak, the taxi driver, was slowly unwinding another tale of an astonishingly obscene happening in his taxi, this being the rule with his fares rather than the exception, then they both clamped shut as soon as Mortimer stepped up to the bar, as if even talk of sex would embarrass him. Griffin, the signal for propriety.

This is not to say the regulars at The Eight Bells were not exceedingly nice to Mortimer, indeed they were, but they also were insultingly correct, as if – in their crafty woggish way – they could sense he didn't have a big one.

Then one day Joyce phoned him at the office, her manner uncharacteristically flirtatious, and asked him to be sure and pick up a tube of vaginal jelly at the chemist's before coming home. The promise of sex, even with Joyce again, was exhilarating, though it did mean he would have to wait while she went into the bathroom to hold her diaphragm up to the light to check against any rubber fatigue since last time. Afterwards she would insist that he bathe. The sheets would be changed. All the same, it might be fun.

Mortimer went to Rapani's, two doors down from The Eight Bells. The old man wasn't happy to see him. Taking him by the arm, he led Mortimer away from his biggest display counter, the one which featured roll upon roll of striptease films, as if even a glimpse of these small boxes might corrupt Mortimer. Hastily getting into his apothecary's white jacket, straightening his tie as he stood pointedly under his framed graduation certificate, the unshaven Rapani rubbed his hands and asked, "And what can I do for you, Mr. Griffin?", somehow suggesting that Mortimer's needs couldn't be more complicated than digestive tablets or perhaps razor blades.

Mortimer told Rapani what he wanted.

"I beg your pardon?"

Mortimer repeated his request and Rapani went to fetch the tube, his manner perplexed, as he wondered if Mortimer knew the stuff wasn't any good for chapped lips.

"Thanks," Mortimer said snidely.

Mortimer did not visit The Eight Bells for the rest of the week. On Monday evening he had no sooner entered the pub than Rapani was at his side. "Did it do the trick?"

The other regulars watched, one or two of them smirking. Mortimer had been found out. In spite of his furled umbrella, he indulged in sexual sports from time to time. This, he thought angrily, is insolence indeed, but he swallowed his indignation. How, he wondered, would Ziggy Spicehandler convert a situation like this to his own advantage?

"It was just the thing, Mr. Rapani. Trouble is I need another tube tonight."

"*Already?*"

The following week Mortimer, walking past Rapani's shop, was startled by a rapping on the window. The old man beckoned Mortimer into the rear of his shop and handed him an unlabeled little box of brown pills. "My own mixture," he said with a wink. "In case you get tired."

Soon Mortimer, trapped into playing out his Ziggy-inspired role, felt obliged to stop at Rapani's at least once a week. He found himself buying tubes of vaginal jelly, diaphragms in all available sizes, prophylactics, and Rapani's very own aphrodisiacs. His stature at The Eight Bells skyrocketed.

"Clean collar, dirty mind," Donnelly observed.

Rapani seldom began to read from his pornographic paperbacks before Mortimer had arrived. "Would you say, Mr. Griffin, that this writer was, ah, accurate?"

The day after *News of the World* revealed that greenbelt suburbanites, seemingly respectable, actually went in for wife-swapping, Gregory, the headwaiter, went out of his way to be friendly. "It's nobody's business but your own," he said.

Wzcedak leaped to Mortimer's defense when the *Sunday Pictorial* did a series on orgies in Debland. "The way they parade their pussy on the King's Road," he said, "there isn't one of them who isn't asking for it."

Mortimer walked tallest in the heady days of the Profumo scandal.

"Here he comes," Rapani would say, raising a glass to him, "the man in the mask."

Wzcedak was openly envious. "He's just lucky enough to have the right accent and –"

"And something else besides," Taylor interrupted, beaming.

With the Denning Report looming over all of them, Donnelly worried for Mortimer's sake. Night after night he insisted on buying him doubles. "Not to worry," he said again and again. "They wouldn't dare to name names."

Mortimer tried to give up his visits to Rapani's shop, but it was no use. Now Rapani brought the goods directly to the pub, forcing them on an unwilling Mortimer. When Mr. Justice Linslow chose to exercise discretion in the case of a famous film star's adultery, Rapani pinched his cheek. "Naughty boy," he said. "*Naughty boy.*"

Then things quieted down until one American magazine after another looked upon London and pronounced it swinging.

"They should have gone to you for an interview. You could have told them what's what."

"Where would I find the time?"

Seventeen

ANOTHER SLEEPLESS, oppressive night, followed by another vile day. Coming out of the toilet, *The Times* folded under his arm, Mortimer ran smack into Joyce, who said in her special icy voice, "Forgot something, didn't we?"

Mortimer was baffled, caught off-balance, until she thrust the tin at him: deodorant spray. "Oh," he said, taking it and returning sheepishly to spray away his smell.

Mortimer wasn't angry. Hygiene, he knew, was her obsession. She simply couldn't tolerate stale food or body odors or a speck on her sheets or insects in the house, even one little fly, which she would hunt down if it took her hours, armed with yet another deadly spray. Joyce's horror of filth extended to secondhand books. She wouldn't let him keep them in the house on the grounds that the previous owner might very well have been a smallpox carrier. Or syph-ridden.

Oh, well. Mortimer dropped Doug off at his wretched school and then continued to Oriole House. In the parking lot alongside Oriole, he ran into the so recently rejuvenated Lord Woodcock.

"Can you take the chair at the conference this morning?" Lord Woodcock asked. "Dino Tomasso is indisposed."

Remembering the two black-suited motorcycle riders, Mortimer asked, "Nothing serious, I hope?"

"Eye trouble. A minor operation. Can you or can you not take the morning –"

"Certainly, sir."

"That's marvelous, Mortimer. We're counting on you, you know."

How well Lord Woodcock looked, Mortimer reflected, as the saintly old man strode to his car.

Only a year ago Lord Woodcock had seemed to be withdrawing into feeble and melancholy dotage, which was easier to comprehend if you remembered the trials and deceptions that British radicals of his generation had endured: Ramsay MacDonald, Spain, the Stalin-Hitler Pact, Hungary, Nye Bevan's untimely death, Nkrumah . . . Mr. Woodcock, as he was then, was understandably disconsolate, even bitter. Almost alone among surviving old socialist hellions of the thirties, he had not been ennobled. Again and again, he was overlooked on the Honours List, increasingly cut off from old comrades who now read *Tribune* and formed ginger groups in the bar at the House of Lords. Then, miraculously, Woodcock was offered a peerage, the Star Maker came into his life, and the transformation in the old man was heartening to behold. At Oriole Press, once more he rode with the young, possibly even a step ahead of them. On the terrace of the House of Lords, he was reinstated to the company of old radicals, once again able to reminisce about the hunger march and even to take the micky out of old Oxbridge enemies, peers of the wrong type, the hereditary type, who had served on the opposite side in the general strike. Old leopards, to hear Lord Woodcock tell it, never change their spots. Defiantly, he explained to Mortimer, the Labour lords rented their ermine at Moss Bros., cracked naughty jokes about the Queen, and insisted on being called by their first names at the party conference. These men who wrote revolutionary pamphlets during the Spanish Civil War now honored their radical past by scribbling anti-establishment graffiti in the peers' toilets.

It's there, Lord Woodcock said, chuckling, for all the other lords to see.

Counting on you. This was the first indication Mortimer had had from Lord Woodcock in months that, like Hy, he was still a candidate for the big job, once Dino Tomasso returned to Hollywood.

Following the morning conference, Mortimer cornered Hy in the hall. "Hy," he pleaded, "let's bury the hatchet. We've been friends for years. I –"

"Any time you're prepared to meet me in the gym, baby, you just let me know."

"Hy, for Christ's sake. It's soon going to be Christ –" Mortimer stopped himself, flushing.

"Christmas? Thank you. Thank you very much," Hy said, slamming his office door after him.

Grudgingly, Joyce started on her shopping for Christmas dinner, going to Monty's, on Haverstock Hill, to place her fruit order well in advance. Fortunately for Monty, who abhorred serving Joyce above all his other customers, he saw her coming this time and quickly bolted out the back door, obliging Archie, the new assistant, to take her order.

"Sprouts?" Archie asked brightly, pencil poised.

Joyce said a pound would do.

"And what about new potatoes? Lovely they are."

"Where are they from?" Joyce demanded suspiciously.

"Italy."

"All right, then. I'll have three pounds."

"Now just feed your eyes on these pineapples. From British Guiana they are. Flown –"

"*Where they are holding Dr. Cheddi Jagan in detention?*"

"I beg your pardon?"

"Would you have any Cuban pineapples?"

"Sorry, no. But let me slice one open for you. These are ever so good."

"That's hardly the point at issue. What about your oranges?"

"Spanish navels. Del-icious. Just in."

"*Spanish* navels. Did you say Spanish fascist navels? Where *is* Monty?"

"Gone out. Oh, look here, we do have some Jaffas, if you like?"

Israeli; now there was a poser. "No." Not since Dayan. "Have you any dates?"

Archie flashed a box of Nigger brand at her.

"Where is Monty? I insist on seeing him."

"Hello, dear! Kiss?"

"Up your ass."

"Oh, my. Bad day?"

"*Übersturmführer* Griffin sucked up to me again at the office. Chicken-shit bastard," Hy said, slipping into a shuffle, his lightning left jab stopping just short of Diana's breasts, "think he doesn't know? One wrong move and I'll flatten him. *Like this*," he said, his right hand suddenly flashing upward toward Diana's chin.

It was a feint. But Diana, taken by surprise, stupidly raised her guard, presenting Hy with a splendid opportunity to bury a right hook in her belly.

"Ooof," went Diana, staggering backward.

"Sucker," Hy hissed, following through with a hammering left to her kidney. A zig, a zag, and then a rat-tat-tat to her ears.

Finally, Diana flicked him off her. "Would you care for a drink before dinner, luv?" she asked warmly.

"I'm going out for dinner."

"Alone?"

Heh-heh. He didn't answer. Instead he shuffled backward, lunging, thrusting, shadowboxing his way into the bathroom. Hy stood on the bath stool, got his mouthpiece out of the medicine cabinet, and growled at his reflection in the mirror.

Hyman Rosen, after all, was merely his goy-given name. Actually, he thought, baring his teeth at the mirror, I am Chaym ben Yussel, one of a great pugilistic line, which includes Black Aby, Cat's Meat Gadzee, Ikey Pig, Ugly Baruk Levy, Little Puss Abrahams, The Yokel Jew Sodicky and, above all, Daniel Mendoza. Mendoza! On January 9, 1788, Hy remembered, the great Mendoza, his ankle broken, fainted from pain, and his archenemy, the brutish Gentleman Dick Humphries, stood over him and shouted, "I have done the Jew!" The hell he had. For on May 6, 1789, Mendoza met Humphries again and reduced the braggardly goy to a bleeding pulp. *Grrr*, went Chaym ben Yussel. *Grrr.*

Oh, dear, Diana thought, recognizing the mood, Hy's Jewish-avenger mood. In such a state, he was inclined to rake the streets, searching for covert Jew-haters; testing people in bus queues, telling them to get fucked; charging after young couples coming out of espresso bars, cursing them in Yiddish; and spitting at old men out walking their dogs. All the same, it wasn't easy for Hy to provoke a fight. Most people had a too-well-developed sense of fair play to hit back at the crazed little man. If he persisted, they made sport of him. But kicking, punching, his flow of obscenities unceasing, Hy was, on occasion, difficult to ignore, and once or twice he was badly mauled.

Grrr.

Mortimer hurried, late again, to catch up with the group he had joined at Paddington Station.

"Have I missed much?" he asked Agnes Laura Ryerson.

"Not to worry," their leader said, intervening, his grin infectious. "But I think you'd best sit this one out and catch your breath, don't you?"

Mortimer had chosen Paddington over Waterloo and other stations after considerable deliberation because he was not likely to run into commuters known to him there, which could be hellishly embarrassing. Not that he hadn't taken precautions. He wore dark glasses and was known to the others as Jim. All the same, he thought, I shouldn't be doing this. God knows what Joyce would think. And she'd be right, as usual. It's commercialized, the brotherly-love bit oozes smugness. The parties, an excuse for the worst sort of promiscuity, are good business and tax deductible. The gift-giving aspect is phony and even most of the cards you get are not from friends but from other firms. Still, Mortimer was a sucker for Christmas. Even before the decorations had gone up on Regent Street, he'd caught the fever.

Last year, damn it, it had been touch and go with Joyce over having a tree. "With so-called Christians bombing Viet Nam? Hypocrisy," Joyce cried. "I had to live with it as a child, but not in my own house."

Mortimer could remember his anguish walking the streets of Hampstead with Doug and staring enviously at the enormous Christmas trees in all the other homes. He decided to have another stab at Joyce. He pointed out that Mrs. Cohen from next door had been giving him filthy looks. "It may seem to the Cohens," he said, "that we don't have a tree in our window because we resent theirs. We are, if only by omission, rebuking them for intruding on the celebration of the birth of our Saviour."

Saviour. Joyce immediately hardened.

"Look here, it's not as if we're bringing a bloody cross into the house. It's just a tree. A pagan symbol."

"Yes, but –"

"Look at it another way. He was a Jew, wasn't he? Naturally I don't accept any of that Immaculate Conception crap –"

"All those women washing his feet *must* have given him an erection."

"Absolutely. But the fact is he was a great Jewish radical leader."

"All the same –"

"Ignoring his birthday, well, it could, you know – it just could be interpreted as anti-Semitic."

So Mortimer got his tree and even Joyce, he liked to think, came to enjoy it.

This year, however, was something else. This year, Mortimer felt, he was already in trouble, walking the most hazardous of tightropes, with three weeks still to go until Christmas. All because of the group he had joined for Agnes Laura Ryerson's sake.

Joyce, encouraged by Dougie, thought he was coming home late from the office two nights a week because he was having it off with Rachel Coleman. His job was to nourish this suspicion without ever offering Joyce proof positive. Joyce would be frightfully displeased if it turned out he was having an affair with another woman, but at least she was colored, which made the prospect interesting, even progressive, and so she would not be humiliated before her friends. Even so, Mortimer was ashamed of the deceptions he had practiced in order to conceal his real lapse and feed Joyce's belief that he was being unfaithful. On Tuesdays and Thursdays after he had taken leave of his group, Mortimer sneaked off to a pub and knocked back two hasty brandies, acquiring a liquored breath. Or he stole a pack of Durex from his hoard, discarded the prophylactics in a convenient toilet and forgot the empty pack in his jacket pocket. He had also once asked Miss Fishman to kiss him on the cheek and then rubbed her lipstick into his handkerchief.

Joyce could not be unstuck from the TV set on Wednesday nights. *Insult* night on BBC-2, with the celebrated inquisitor, Digby Jones. Last Wednesday Dig had made a young Tory backbencher, one of the most independent and progressive in the House, his target. He was shown, by astute questioning, to be something less than an idealist. "He is," Dig asked, turning to his studio audience, signaling for what had become the weekly battle cry, "what, fans?"

"*No better than the rest of us.*"

Tonight, which was to bring Joyce the last *Insult* before Christmas, was vintage stuff. Somehow or other tricksy old Dig had cajoled Sister Theresa, a nun renowned for her goodness, to appear on his show. Breaking Sister Theresa down slowly, leading her on by paying tribute to the fact she lived in self-imposed slum conditions in Brixton, taking in old lags, giving succor to meths men, maintaining an orphanage for unwanted children, he suddenly lashed out at her: "But can you tell me, Sister, if you have ever had intercourse with a man?"

"No."

"With another woman, then?"

"No."

"Isn't it possible, then, that your *goodness*, this meddling into the lives of the poor, is not divinely motivated, but borne of sexual frustration?"

"I think not, Mr. Jones."

"You think not." Dig scowled at the studio audience, choking their laughter. "But if one may lapse into street argot, you're not getting it regular, are you?"

"No."

"Tell me this: Does helping unwed mothers and alcoholics, taking the unwanted to your bosom, metaphorically speaking, make you feel good?"

"It makes me feel useful."

"Does it make you feel good?"

"Well, it doesn't make me feel bad, certainly."

"In other words, helping the oppressed affords you . . . pleasure?"

Sister Theresa sighed; she nodded weakly.

"Would it be altogether unfair, then, to describe you not

as suppressed – *but as a sexually diverted nymphomaniac?* A pornographer of the do-good?"

As the unlying camera zoomed in on Sister Theresa's sobbing face, Dig demanded, "What is she, fans?"

"*As shitty as we are!*"

Winding up for the Christmas break, Dig looked into the cameras and repeated his invitation to the Star Maker to appear on *Insult*. Five previous invitations had gone unanswered, even though the Star Maker no longer had a valid excuse for his absence, the sight of his bad eye having been miraculously restored.

Swaggering down Kensington Church Street, his shoulders bent forward, his bloodshot eyes narrowed and menacing, fists ready inside his belted mac, Hy Rosen was totally unaware that he was being shadowed by a towering shiksa who held a field hockey stick inside her coat. A tall, gray-haired man came strolling toward him. Immediately Hy slammed into him, using his shoulder as a wedge.

"You drunken idiot," the man said. "Look where you're going."

"Drunken idiot? I'm as good as you are. Better, probably."

"I beg your pardon?"

"Why, you fucking anti-Semitic whoremaster. You –"

Hy ducked under the tall, gray-haired man's clumsy right and, eyes jammed shut, let rip with a looping left of his own.

"Oooo," the gray-haired man moaned, sinking to the pavement.

Heh-heh. I've done in another Jew-baiter, Chaym ben Yussel thought, unperturbed to look up and see three teenagers come charging toward him. "Hey, we saw you," one of the boys shouted.

"Come and get me," Hy called back, leading with his left.

But the boys ran past him, round the corner. "Hey! Hey you! Stop!"

Chicken, Hy thought, immediately giving chase. "Here I am, you bastards! Here I am!"

"Joyce? I'm home."

But she was already asleep. So Mortimer settled down on the sofa with his *Evening Standard*, where he read that the Star currently in London filming for the Star Maker had once more refused to see reporters about his rumored romance with a famous British duchess. As it happened, one of the Star's old movies was showing on TV, the late movie, and so Mortimer flicked it on. It was uncanny, truly amazing, Mortimer thought, but looking from the Star's photograph in the *Standard* to his fifteen-year-old image on the TV screen, he hardly seemed to have aged at all in the years between.

Following the movie, Mortimer stayed up for the news, which was how he first found out that the dreary Labour politician, who was the subject of the first biography in the Our Living History series, had killed himself, with publication day only ten days off. The politician had been found dead in his Hampstead flat. He had hanged himself with a black silk stocking from a chandelier in a room replete with two-way mirrors, rhino whips, dildos, and other erotic paraphernalia.

God damn it. Dino Tomasso, stupidly lucky, Mortimer thought, had obviously got himself a best seller, but he was bound to burn his fingers with the next title in the series, the faded film star's biography.

Eighteen

"It's going to be published," Agnes Laura Ryerson said, defiantly pleased. "By the Free Presbytery of Glasgow. Their *Annual Report on Public Questions, Religions, and Morals*. Do you mind if I read a point or two aloud to you?"

"Oh, please do," Joyce said icily.

Mortimer hastily freshened his drink.

"All must be prostrated," Miss Ryerson read, "before the great Hedonistic Juggernaut; this has been the year of the Parliamentary campaign to stamp the foul brand of Sodom upon the nation's brow and it has been the year of Parliamentary activity to have the future of our island race in part decided in the broiler-house minds of eugenists and abortionists; it has been the year of the meeting of Canterbury and Rome and it will be too much to hope that it will be abortive." Miss Ryerson paused; she looked over the rims of her glasses to see if Mortimer and Joyce were being attentive. "The quality of our culture is signalised by the fact that the accolades of royal recognition are given to maestros of moronic music. What this represents is cultural cretinism –"

"I don't mean to be rude, Miss Ryerson," Mortimer interrupted, "but I'm afraid we really must run."

"Oh, didn't you know?" Joyce asked, beaming. "Miss Ryerson is coming with us."

"*What?*"

"I've already invited her."

Mortimer refilled his glass and promptly drained it. "We're going to be late," he said gloomily.

And they were. Excuse me, beg your pardon, Mortimer muttered, leading Joyce and Agnes Laura Ryerson to their seats in the Beatrice Webb auditorium, which was gaily tricked out with reams of colored ribbons, balloons, and mistletoe, for the Christmas play. A rosy-cheeked boy skipped across the stage waving a placard which read PHILOSOPHY IN THE BEDROOM. He was followed by a giggly, plump ten-year-old girl with another placard: DIALOGUE THE FOURTH.

Mortimer focused on the stage, where four nude ten-year-olds (two boys, two girls) were frolicking on an enormous bed. The effect was comic, making Mortimer recall an old *Saturday Evening Post* cover by Norman Rockwell, which had shown a freckled little girl sitting at her mother's dressing table, the gap between her teeth showing as she puckered her lips to try on her mother's lipstick.

The boy playing Dolmance said, "I see but one way to terminate this ridiculous ceremony: look here, Chevalier, we are educating this pretty girl, we are teaching her all a little girl of her age should know and, the better to instruct her, we join – we join – we join –"

"Some practice to theory," the prompter hissed.

"– some practice to theory. She must have a tableau dressed for her: it must feature a prick –"

"Louder, please," a parent behind Mortimer called out.

"– a prick discharging, that's where presently we are; would you like to serve as a model?"

Le Chevalier de Mirvel, played by a big black West Indian boy, whom the audience desperately wanted to do well, responded, biting back his laughter, "Surely, the proposal is too flattering to refuse, and Mademoiselle has the charms that will quickly guarantee the desired lesson's effects."

Madame de Saint-Ange, a gawky child, all ribs and knees it seemed, squealed, "Then let's go on: to work!"

Which was when they fell to wrestling on the bed, le Chevalier de Mirvel, to judge by his laughter, being the most ticklish of the four.

"Oh, indeed," Eugénie hollered, "'tis too much; you abuse my inexperience to such a degree . . ."

The West Indian boy kissed Eugénie.

"Smack, smack," Dolmance called out, for Miss Tanner had encouraged them to improvise.

"Here comes the mushy stuff," Madame de Saint-Ange pitched in, alienating herself from her part. She was, after all, only playing Madame de Saint-Ange. For real, as Miss Tanner had explained, she was Judy Faversham.

"Oh, God!" the West Indian boy hollered. "What fresh, what sweet attractions!"

Agnes Laura Ryerson's face went the color of ashes. Behind Mortimer, a man demanded gruffly of his wife, "When does Gerald come on stage?"

"Quiet, James."

Yet another father voiced his displeasure. "There aren't enough parts."

"It's a classic, Cyril."

"All the same, it's a school play. There should be more parts. It's jolly unfair to the other children."

Mortimer's attention was gripped by the free-for-all on stage. Puzzling over the nude, goose-pimply children entwined on the bed, he wondered, le Chevalier de Mirvel aside, which leg, what rib cage, belonged to whom. Dolmance squealed, "I have seen girls younger than this sustain still more massy pricks: with courage and patience life's greatest obstacles are surmounted –"

"Here come the clichés," the man behind Mortimer said, groaning.

"'Tis madness to think one must have a child deflowered

by only very small pricks. I hold the contrary view, that a virgin should be delivered to none but the vastest engines to be had . . ."

Suddenly the stage lights dimmed and the bed was abandoned to le Chevalier de Mirvel and Eugénie. Secondary lights brightened and behind the free-floating gauze that formed the rear bedroom wall there magically loomed the boys and girls of the second form, Doug's form, cupids as it were, humming a nervy, bouncy tune and carrying flickering, star-shaped lights. There was enthusiastic applause and only one harsh cry of "Derivative!" from the man behind Mortimer, as the kids filed on stage and formed a circle round the bed, where le Chevalier de Mirvel and Eugénie still tussled. Then, taking the audience completely by surprise, a fairy godmother, wearing a tall pointed hat, all sparkly and wound round and round in shimmering blue chiffon, was suspended in midair over the bed. The fairy godmother was none other than Mr. Yasha Krashinsky, who taught Expressive Movement at Beatrice Webb House.

Deafening applause greeted the rotund, dangling Yasha Krashinsky, a touching measure of support, as it was widely known that he had soon to appear at the Old Bailey, charged with importuning outside Covent Garden. While the second-form choir hummed, Yasha Krashinsky chanted, "Le Chevalier de Mirvel is wilting. Our fair Eugénie is fading fast. They will only make it, grown-ups, if you believe in the cure-all powers of the orgasm. Grown-ups, do you believe in the orgasm?"

"Yes!"

The pitch of the humming heightened. Yasha Krashinsky chanted, "The young virgin and her lover cannot hear you. Louder, grown-ups. Do you believe in the orgasm?"

"*Yes! Yes! Yes!*"

Blackness on stage. The throbbing of drums. Squeals from

the bed. One of the boys from the second-form choir took a step forward, raised his arms aloft, and shouted: "Hip! Hip!"

"*Hurrah!*" returned the choir.

"Hip! Hip!"

"*Hurrah!*"

A spotlight picked out the fairy godmother, Yasha Krashinsky, as he was lowered with a clunk on stage; and poured a flask of red paint into a bucket.

"*Now she is a woman,*" the choir sang to the tune of "Pomp and Circumstance." "*Eugénie's a woman now.*"

Once the play was done, the children skipped off to the dining hall, where choc-ices, a conjurer, and a Popeye cartoon show awaited them. The adults remained in the auditorium, where they were served vin rosé and cheese squares. Dr. Booker, Yasha Krashinsky, and finally Miss Lilian Tanner, mounted the stage to shouts of "Bravo," and the meeting was called to order. Mortimer was immensely encouraged to discover that he was not alone in being rather put off by the Beatrice Webb House production of *Philosophy in the Bedroom*. He was in a minority, a reactionary minority, but he was not alone. As the meeting progressed beyond niceties, Mortimer was heartened to see other parents come to the boil. The play was not the issue. It was, however, symptomatic of what some parents felt had come to ail the school.

Francis Wharton, the enlightened TV producer, began by saying he had always voted Socialist; he deplored censorship in any shape or form, on either side of the so-called Iron Curtain; Victorian double standards were anathema to him; but all the same he thought it a bit much that just because his thirteen-year-old daughter was the only girl in the fifth form to stop at petting –

"Shame," somebody called out.

– *heavy* petting –

The objector shrugged, unimpressed.

– was no reason for her to come home with a scarlet *T* for "tease" painted on her bosom.

This brought Lady Gillian Horsham, the Oxfam organizer, to her feet. Lady Horsham wished for more colored neighbors in Lowndes Square. She had, she said, found the play on the twee side here and there, but, on balance, most imaginative.

"Yes, yes," Dr. Booker interrupted bitingly, "but?"

Lady Horsham explained that her daughter, also in the fifth form, but not so cripplingly inhibited as the previous speaker's child –

"Hear! Hear!"

– had already been to the London Clinic to be fitted with a diaphragm.

"That's the stuff!"

"Good girl!"

But, she continued, but, wasn't it all rather premature? Not, mind you, that she was a prude. But, as they were all socialists, it seemed to her irresponsible that while their sisters in Africa and India were in such desperate need of diaphragms –

"Not germane," somebody hollered.

Yes, it was germane, Lady Horsham continued. But look at it another way, if you must. Parents were already overburdened with spiraling fees, the cost of summer and winter uniforms, hockey sticks, cricket bats, and what not. Was it fair that they should now also have to fork out for new diaphragms each term as, let's face it, these were growing girls? Couldn't the girls of the fifth form, without psychological damage –

"Your question, please?"

– without risk, practice *coitus interruptus?*

"Spoilsport!"

"Reactionary!"

Dr. Booker beamed at his people, gesturing for silence. "If I may make a positive point, there is no reason why the tuck shop co-op, which already sells uniforms the girls have outgrown to younger students, could not also dispose of diaphragms that have begun to pinch, *so long as the transaction was not tarnished by the profit motive*."

Next to speak up, Tony Latham, the outspoken Labour backbencher, explained that while it certainly did not trouble him personally that his boy masturbated daily, immediately following the Little Fibber Bra commercials on ITV, it was quite another matter when his parents, up from the country, were visiting. Latham's parents, it was necessary to understand, were the product of a more inhibited, censorious age: it distressed them, rather, to see their only grandchild playing with himself on the carpet, while they were taking tea.

"Your question, Mr. Latham?"

Could it be put to Yasha Krashinsky, overworked as he is, that he keep the boys for five minutes after Expressive Movement class, and have them masturbate before they come home?

"But I do," Yasha put in touchily. "I do, my dear chap."

Other, more uncompromisingly radical parents now demanded their say. There could be no backsliding at Beatrice Webb House. "You begin," a lady said, "by forbidding masturbation in certain rooms or outside prescribed hours and next thing you know the children, our children, are driven back into locked toilets to seek their pleasure, and still worse have developed a sense of guilt about auto-stimulation."

"Or," another mother said, looking directly at Lady Horsham, "you allow one greedy-guts in the fourth form to hold on to her precious little hymen and next thing out goes fucking in the afternoon."

There followed a long and heated discussion on the play, its larger meanings within meanings, and then a debate on Beatrice Webb House finances, co-op shares, and needs and plans for the future, if – as Dr. Booker put it, winding up to a standing ovation – LBJ was going to allow us a future. Some compromises were grudgingly agreed to. Diaphragms, for instance, would be made optional until a girl reached the sixth form. On the other hand, Dr. Booker absolutely refused to stream girls into classes of those who did and those who didn't. It would be heartless, he said feelingly, to stamp a girl of twelve frigid for the rest of her life. Some, if not all, late developers might grow up to surpass seemingly more avid girls in sexual appetite. "Thursday's heavy petter, properly encouraged," he said, "might develop into Friday's nympho."

Mortimer, and three other hard-core reactionaries managed to take over the interview-and-appointments committee. There were, at the moment, two teaching vacancies, one in the second form, Doug's form.

"That's for me," Miss Ryerson said.

England needs me. "Oh, my God, no, Miss Ryerson. I couldn't."

"*You must.*"

"But –"

"Don't you worry about Agnes Laura Ryerson. I'll show them a thing or two."

"Yes, Miss Ryerson."

Nineteen

DINO TOMASSO, SOMEWHAT subdued, wearing a patch over his left eye, came out of the London Clinic and returned to work in time to gloat over the success of the first title in the Our Living History series, already gone into a second printing.

More luck than brains, Mortimer thought grudgingly, but he let it pass. He had a more pressing matter to cope with. For, beginning with his next "Reading for Pleasure" lecture, Jacob Shalinsky contrived to make life a misery for him.

"Ah, Mr. Griffin, I may have misinterpreted you, of course, but it seems to me you place T. S. Eliot among the great writers of our age. Do you think it possible, Mr. Griffin, that anti-Semitism goes hand in hand with literary greatness? Answer me that."

Shalinsky brought I. M. Sinclair with him.

"Griffin, it is a historical fact that when Sholom Aleichem came to New York, Mark Twain was among the first to greet him. 'I want to meet you,' he said, 'because I understand I am an American Sholom Aleichem.' "

"Your question, please, Dr. Sinclair."

"How come, then, that we have been asked to read *Huckleberry Finn*, but not *The Adventures of Mottel?*"

I. M. Sinclair brought Daniels, who came with Katansky.

Katansky took his brother-in-law Shapiro along with him. Shapiro opened his *Daily Mail*, licked a pencil, and filled in the time doing the crossword puzzles.

Another newcomer, a man called Michaelson, sat alone in a corner. He was incredibly pale, an emaciated man of fifty or so, with large staring eyes and a thin mouth; he twitched. Beside him there sat two more of Shalinsky's people, possibly father and son, who were given to whispering together conspiratorially. The younger of the two, still in his twenties, wore a dirty windbreaker. He needed a haircut badly and was constantly jerking his head back to get the hair out of his eyes. The older man wore a shiny gray suit. Whenever Mortimer paused in his lecture, riffling through his notes, he smiled contemptuously, nudging the younger man. And the younger man, responding to the prod, would begin to laugh, but between his teeth, making a small noise that sounded *tssst-tssst-tssst.*

Fumbling, in a foul temper, Mortimer would hurtle onward, skipping whole pages of carefully prepared notes. Even so, he was clearly never finished with his lecture before the dreaded question-and-answer period began.

"And now, Griffin," I. M. Sinclair would demand, shooting up from his seat, "how about a little give and take?"

"Well, I –"

"Speak Hebrew," the pale emaciated man called out, his head lowered, the face hidden behind trembling hands. "Say it in our own language."

Next Katansky demanded to be heard. Slowly he shed his glasses, dropped them into his breast pocket, and wiped his eyes. "First of all, Griffin," he said, "let me say your lecture tonight was A-1 – *and I'm a hard man to please.* In your command of the English language, Griffin, you are a field marshal while I am a mere corporal. Of course it's true I speak many other languages," he added, shrugging his shoulders, "but . . . anyway my question runs as follows. My son, Griffin, is studying at Leeds University and he wishes to become a novelist. What – I would like to know – must he do to join the old boy's network and how much can he expect to earn after five years?"

Shalinsky sprung to his feet. "Katansky, that is hardly germane to the –"

"Did I ask you or the professor?"

"Katansky's got a point," I. M. Sinclair called out sharply. "If Griffin wishes to answer his mundane question . . ."

"Well, Mr. Katansky, a lot would depend on your son's ability and –"

"Of my son's ability there is no question."

"– and, um, the content of your son's novel. You see –"

"*Shmutz*," Daniels shouted at Katansky.

"Pardon?"

"Filth. Today nothing sells like filth."

Shalinsky asked Mortimer which ten books he would take to a desert island. Grudgingly, Mortimer made up a list for him.

"Three of them are by Jewish authors," Shalinsky said, turning to the others. "That's *something*, anyway."

Katansky wanted to know if Mortimer approved of book clubs. I. M. Sinclair, if he thought art could survive under capitalism. Daniels asked in a shy whisper if, speaking as a Gentile, he thought the novel was dead.

"What is the name of a river in France with five letters?"

"Are you trying to be funny, Shapiro?"

"The Seine."

Tssst-tsst-tssst.

"It doesn't fit."

"Try the Loire."

I. M. Sinclair sprang to his feet. "If one were to take your feeble word for it, Griffin, then Graham Greene is one of the leading novelists of our age."

Tssst.

"What does Graham Greene say to make himself such a paragon? He says the banks are run by Jews and that the sons of these Jewish bankers rape Irish virgins –"

"Irish *and a virgin*. Find me one!"

Tssst-tssst.

"– and, furthermore, among the Gentiles there is sin and suicide. This is profound? This I can verify on any street corner."

"Now wait a minute," Mortimer began. "Hold on –"

Michaelson cupped his hands to his mouth. "*Hebrew is the most beautiful tongue known to man. Speak it!*"

"He's only a goy, for Christ's sake! How can he speak it?"

Shalinsky rose to his full height, cigarette ashes dribbling onto his jacket. "*He is not a goy.*"

Twenty

TELEGRAM:

THE POOR ARE ALWAYS WITH US. ZIGGY COMES BUT ONCE A SEASON. ARRIVING THE 20TH. SPICEHANDLER.

Ziggy Spicehandler's second coming called for preparations both intricate and varied. Fifteen minutes after Ziggy's telegram arrived, Mortimer set to rearranging his books haphazardly on the shelves. He didn't want Ziggy, his grin taunting, to say yet again, "So that's the kind of cat you've become? All the French novels on one shelf and the Americana in a special bookcase. How tidy!" Then Mortimer went through his books one by one, erasing his name from any volume he had written it into. Settling back weary but happy, at 2 A.M., to consider his labors, he lit a cigarette and, wincing inwardly, practiced flicking ashes on the carpet. Oh well, he thought, at least it's going to be worse for Joyce. Liberated Joyce, hygienic Joyce, who would be outraged by each and every one of Ziggy's personal habits. Beer and belches for breakfast, cigarettes squashed into the uncongealed bacon fat on his plate. Coca-Cola tins opened with a spurt and then abandoned anywhere, making rims on the dining room table, leaving sticky spots on the sideboard. Old friends, sometimes strange girls, brought home unannounced for lunch. Afternoon naps, Spicehandler's daily ziz, on the living room sofa. Ziggy flapping barefoot through the house, picking his toes as he watched television. Migod, Mortimer thought, exhilarated by the effect this was bound to have on Joyce, Ziggy drinking or smoking pot in bed, a fire hazard, would be sufficient to make her grind her teeth.

The magazines!

Mortimer caught a glimpse of *The New Yorker* on the hassock. Must remember to drop it and *Time*, he thought, and in their place order *Playboy* and *Evergreen*. Mortimer, rising to conceal his back file of *Which*, cursed himself for having so recently put his small garden in bourgeois, suburban order. This coming Sunday he would have to undo a month's systematic labor; strewing junk (a slap in the face to his neat conformist neighbors) about the garden. Doug's pissy old mattress heaved on the grass would be a nice touch. The car needs washing, Mortimer thought. Good. The dented boot was especially lucky; it would surely demonstrate to Ziggy a healthy indifference to possessions.

Ziggy, good old Ziggy, there would be so much to talk about. He would tell him about his troubles with that lunatic Shalinsky, who thought he was Jewish, and how Rachel Coleman, not to brag, had the hots for him. They would speculate about the legendary, undying Star Maker, Dino Tomasso, and the altogether baffling Polly Morgan. To Ziggy, a bottle of brandy between them, Mortimer might even confess his anxieties about the size of his cock.

Ah, Ziggy.

Ziggy Spicehandler, née Gerald Spencer, was six years younger than Mortimer. His grandfather, Meir Spicehandler, had emigrated to Leeds from Odessa, and opened a tailor shop in the Leylands. His father, Cyril, had changed the family name to Spencer, married a Yorkshire shiksa, and over the years developed the basement tailor shop into an immensely successful clothing factory. Ziggy had not immediately reverted to the old family name. He was known as Gerald Spencer at Rugby and Oxford. Oxford, where Ziggy was sent down in his second year, for systematically picking up homosexuals and extracting love letters from them for the purpose of blackmail. Ziggy's profits, though not inconsiderable, were hardly the point. In a brilliantly argued defense, later published as a broadside, Ziggy explained that he had acted as he had to demonstrate that if God were dead, everything was indeed lawful. In Paris, a year later, Ziggy published his first novel, a pornographic tour de force. The lechers and harlots in Ziggy's fiction, the perverts and whoremasters, went by the names of his mother, his aunts and uncles, his *baba*, his *zeyda*, and Jewish community leaders in Leeds. It was in fact rather more than just another novel of rebellion against Jewish middle-class values. "I acted out the family's fantasies for them," Ziggy was still fond of saying. But Ziggy's father, to whom the novel was dedicated, never got to read the book. He got no further than the dedication, which read:

FOR DADDY
But For The Grace Of Whose Cock,
Ever Big and Stiff . . .

Even at RADA, a few years later, Ziggy still went by the name of Gerald Spencer. However, coming out of RADA in 1954, Gerald, as he still was, discovered that his Anglicized name, his expensive middle-class education, his knowledge of stage classics, Latin, Greek, his unexcelled elocution, had all contrived to make him singularly ill-equipped for life in modern England. Ziggy, making the rounds of the agents, soon found out he was only fit for comic relief parts in the new school of the kitchen sink. In 1954, all the real people were working-class.

So Ziggy went to Paris, where he fell in with the Americans

in St. Germain des Prés; from there, logically, he drifted to Greenwich Village by way of Ibiza and Mexico, and then even as far north as Canada, where he flourished briefly, impregnating French Canadian girls, raising babies to the age of three months, and then selling them to childless couples in Manhattan. Settled in New York again, he soon overcame the handicap of his upper-crust British accent sufficiently to return to London, a hipster, knowledgeable about jazz talk, Yiddish slang and drugs. He was reborn Ziggy Spicehandler, a self-confessed Renaissance Man, poet, film maker, actor and painter.

Twenty-One

TSSST-TSSST.

"Griffin, a question, please. It –"

"Not now, Mr. Shalinsky."

Shapiro brought Segal, and Segal dragged Sam Klein and his boy along to the lecture. Whenever Mortimer made a little joke in passing, Sam Klein slipped two fingers into his mouth and whistled, beckoning for applause. Flushed and stumbling, raising his voice against whispers and yawns, Mortimer rumbled on and on.

"Louder," barked a voice in the back row. So Mortimer spoke louder.

"What does he say?" somebody called Takifman shouted.

Mortimer waited while Segal translated what he had said into Yiddish.

"Nonsense," Takifman said.

"Ah, Griffin, a question please –"

"This is not the time, Mr. Shalinsky."

"– It seems to me that in your appreciation of Shakespeare –"

"May he rest in peace," Daniels said.

"– we have so far failed to discuss one of the bard's major plays, *The Merchant of Venice*. I wonder if you could tell me why?"

"Look here, Shalinsky, I do not intend to put up with your insolence for another minute. There are other problems besides the Jewish problem. This is not the Jewish Thought Literary Society, but my class in Reading for Pleasure. I'll run it however I please and damn your perverse Jewish soul."

"We'll see about that," Shalinsky said, sitting down. "Won't we, *chaverim?*"

Tssst.

The following morning Mortimer discovered, to his consternation, that Dino Tomasso had hit it lucky again. Three days before the second title in the Our Living History series, the biography of the faded film star, was to be published, the star died from an overdose of heroin. He left a note saying he had done himself in because he had got a fifteen-year-old girl with child, his granddaughter as a matter of fact.

Tomasso asked Mortimer to stay behind after the morning conference. "Mort, I'm not exactly sure how to put this," he began, when the phone rang, interrupting him.

It was Frankfort on the line, the efficiency team. They told Tomasso, Mortimer gathered, that the next title in the Our Living History series was to be a biography of a most attractive political crusader. A junior minister in the Labour Government, who was at present campaigning for a new and possibly punitive tax on gambling casinos.

"But he's so young," Tomasso protested.

Somebody on the other end of the line began to shout in German. The book, Tomasso was told, had already been commissioned. Tomasso hung up, sweaty, agitated. "I must be getting soft," he muttered.

"I don't understand."

Tomasso, who had quite forgotten Mortimer was still in the office, started. "Never mind," he said, opening a file on his desk.

Letters from Katansky, Takifman, Segal and others in Mortimer's "Reading for Pleasure" class had arrived in the first post, complaining about him. It was also rumored that a position demanding Mortimer's expulsion was being circulated by a noted general practitioner from Golders Green, one I. M. Sinclair. "It's well-known that Oriole sponsors those lectures. All this could be bad for our image," Tomasso said, "if it ever leaked out to the newspapers."

"The newspapers? Who in the hell would take such a story to them?"

"Mort, are you an anti-Semite?"

"No."

"Are you Jewish, then?"

Mortimer leaped to his feet.

"It's a joke," Tomasso said, "just a joke, for Christ's sake!"

A buzzer went, interrupting, and Tomasso was summoned to his outer office. Quickly Mortimer scooted round the desk and opened the file, usually locked in the safe, on the Our Living History series. He read two pages, then another. Oh, my God, he thought, no, it can't be true. Biting back nausea, he shut the file.

"Well," Tomasso asked, returning to the office, "what are we going to do about it?"

"About what?" Mortimer asked in a small voice.

"These letters. The petition. Your pal Shalinsky."

"I'm not sure . . ."

"The Star Maker abhors bad publicity."

"Does he?"

"Tell you what. You sleep on it," Tomasso said, brushing an imaginary bit of dust off the Our Living History file, "we'll talk about it again first thing in the morning. Why, you look terrible, Mort. Anything wrong?"

"Yes," Mortimer said, averting his eyes from the file. "I must speak with the Star Maker."

"Easier said than done. The Star Maker is off to America the day after tomorrow."

The instant Mortimer had gone, Tomasso, enormously pleased with himself, got on the phone to the Star Maker. "Well, well," he said, "I was right about Griffin after all."

"How's that?"

"I left the Our Living History file out –"

"*You what?*"

"On purpose, Star Maker. He couldn't wait to bury his nose in it."

"You Goddamn fool."

"Me, I'm a fool. Weren't you the one who said, when I first warned you about him, that he was just another intellectual? Typical sour grapes?"

"All right. Griffin strikes me as an ambitious young man. I'm sure I can handle him."

"I wonder. He's got integrity, you know."

"Has he? Oh, Dino, I think you ought to come over here. I've got some wonderful, wonderful news."

"For me?"

"You said it to me first, Dino. Remember?"

It can't be true, Mortimer thought, it's just too incredible.

After the carol service with Agnes Laura Ryerson and the others at Paddington Station, Mortimer did not go directly to his lecture. He went from pub to pub, drinking heavily.

"Ah, Griffin, there is something I would like to ask you –"

"There is something I would like to ask you, Mr. Shalinsky," Mortimer said, swaying a little.

"And what is that, Griffin?"

"Do me a favor, Shalinsky. I've only got four more lectures to give. Don't come. Stay away. You and your aggressive friends."

"What?"

"I'd be grateful to you for the rest of my life."

"But your lectures are marvelous, Griffin. A delight."

"Some delight."

"Why, some of your epigrams I have marked down in my notebook to cherish. To memorize, Mr. Griffin."

"I've got news for you, Shalinsky. They're not mine. I stole them from my professor at Upper Canada."

"So what? Didn't Shakespeare –"

"May he rest in peace."

"– steal from Thomas Kyd? The oral tradition, Griffin, is –"

"Shalinsky, I beg of you . . . you and your friends . . . quit my lectures."

"Absolutely no."

Emptied, undone, Mortimer said, "all right, then. I regret to announce that this class is now adjourned. There was to have been one more lecture before the Christmas break. I hereby cancel it."

Stunned faces here and there. Some angry ones too.

"As I will not be seeing you again before the Christmas holidays, I'd like to take this opportunity of wishing you a Merry Christmas and a Happy New Year." Smiling sardonically, he added, "And to those among you who do not celebrate the birth of our Saviour may I, in any case, wish you a Happy New Year."

Turning smartly, Mortimer started out of the lecture room.

Tsst-tsst-tsst.

Mortimer fled, fled as far as the nearest pub, then continued to another, another and another.

"Hullo."

"Hullo, my darling."

Joyce, worse luck, had not only elected to wait up for Mortimer, but she was tricked out in what he glumly recognized as her seduction robes. A blue chiffon negligée.

"Would you be kind enough to pour me a drink?" Mortimer asked wearily.

"Certainly."

Then she was in his arms, rubbing against him, kissing him with uncharacteristic passion.

"My darling," she said unconvincingly.

It was astonishing – humiliating – but Mortimer was unable to manage an erection. My God. This, he grasped instinctively, was more than drunkenness. What Mortimer had secretly feared for years had come to pass at last. He was not only small, but impotent as well.

"You're crying. Oh, my darling, please."

Rocking his head in her arms, smiling inwardly, Joyce understood that she now had the ultimate proof. Mortimer was incapable because he had just come from the other woman, Rachel Coleman.

"Sh," she said merrily, licensed, she thought. "Sh," she said, stroking his head. "Sh."

Twenty-Two

MORTIMER AND JOYCE WERE at the breakfast table when the doorbell rang.

"Ziggy! Its Ziggy!" Mortimer embraced his old friend. "God damn it, Ziggy, but I'm glad to see you. If only you knew how glad!"

"Um, sure," Ziggy said, disengaging himself, glancing apprehensively at Joyce over Mortimer's shoulder, wondering what manner of reception she would give him. "Look, man, I've only got French bread on me. Like there's this taxi waiting . . ."

Mortimer hurried outside to settle with the taxi driver.

"Coffee?" Joyce asked noncommittally.

"You're looking very well," Ziggy said.

Which was when Joyce realized that she was still wearing her chiffon negligée. "Oh, dear," she said, her cheeks reddening. "Excuse me a minute."

Joyce returned buttoned up to the throat in her brown velvet dressing gown, hand in hand with Doug.

Ziggy grinned at the boy. "Remember your Uncle Ziggy, kiddo?"

"Y-y-yes."

Mortimer poured Ziggy a vodka-on-the-rocks and explained, "This is terrible, Ziggy, but I must go to the office this morning. There's something I simply must straighten out. Look, don't go out, will you? I'll hurry back."

Ziggy nodded graciously. Joyce poured him another coffee.

"What's bugging Mortimer? I've never seen him look so lousy."

"I don't want to talk about it," Joyce said, pushing her chair back from the table and fleeing to the kitchen.

Oi, Ziggy thought, oi, as he heard sobs coming from the bedroom. He finished his coffee and poured himself another cup. There was no household money in the coffee tin. Or the sugar canister. Suddenly Doug stood before him, beaming.

"Daddy's got a popsie," Doug said.

"Mortimer! No shit?"

"Quite," Doug said, getting into his coat. "I think it's rather super, don't you?"

"You cutting out, kid?"

"I thought perhaps you'd like to speak to Mother alone."

"I see."

"I won't be back until three. I haven't got a key so I'll have to ring, actually."

"You're a swinger, kid. *Ciao.*"

"*Ciao.*"

Ziggy rubbed his jaw pensively. He slipped a hand under his armpit, withdrew it, and smelled. Foo! He reached for the kitchen towel, wet it, and wiped under both armpits. He found the cutlery drawer, took out a paring knife, and methodically cleaned his fingernails. Then Ziggy went into the hall, studied himself in the mirror, and ruffled his hair. He started for the bedroom, where she was still sobbing fitfully. Wait! Ziggy lowered his hand into his underwear, took a good grab, and had a whiff of his fingers. Pig! He went back for the kitchen towel.

"May I come in?" he asked in his tippy-toe voice.

Naturally she didn't answer. So Ziggy turned the door handle softly and sat down beside her on the bed, where she lay face down. "Joyce?" He began to stroke her tenderly, from top to bottom. "Stop crying, Joyce." He raked her more slowly now, lingering where it was warmest. "I hope you're not contemplating the bitchy thing, the obvious thing . . ."

"What?" Joyce turned over sharply, arching away from his hand, the five fevered fingers. "You bastard," she said.

Ziggy nodded, emphatically agreeing. "You're the only one," he said, "who has always been able to see right through me."

"Oh, you're rotten," she said, as he reached for the top button of her dressing gown. "Mortimer looks up to you. There's nobody he admires more."

"Yes, yes. And who could blame you, poor kid, if you wanted to get even with him."

Mortimer found Dino Tomasso in a state, all but frothing with anger. "Yes? What is it, Mort?"

"Before the Star Maker flies back to America, I must speak with him. I insist, Dino."

Pacing, favoring his artificial leg, Tomasso turned his unseeing eye on Mortimer. "The Star Maker isn't flying back to America tomorrow. He's going into the Clinic. He's mad, certifiably insane."

"I don't understand."

"What do you understand? Shmuck."

"Rather more than you think."

"But what about me? He promised me. I've got no sons, he said. You're my son, Dino. He put it in writing. Now the old bastard is going into the Clinic. I tell you, I could cut my tongue out. If I had a knife . . ."

"Why?"

Dino Tomasso sank into his chair. "I never should have blown my stack. No matter what, I never should have talked back to the Star Maker." All at once Tomasso was weeping. "Go now," he said, banging his head against his desk. "Go now."

"Is the Star Maker sick?"

"Sick? If he pulls it off, we'll all be sick. He can't," Tomasso said, knocking wood. "No, no, even the Star Maker, Blessed Be His Name, can't."

"Can't *what?*"

"Can't what?" Tomasso brought a three-fingered hand fearfully to his mouth. "I didn't say it. I never told you what. Isn't that the truth?"

"Yes."

"Oh, my God, what's come over me? Sit down, Griffin. Stop grilling me. Let me get a grip on myself." Tomasso leaned back in his chair, his eyes shut. "Go know," he said over and over again.

"Dino, I must speak with the Star Maker."

"You've seen the Our Living History file?"

Mortimer nodded.

"Big eyes! Snooper! Spy! Mort, I'm going to do you a favor."

Mortimer waited.

"The picture's finished. They wound up yesterday. You know that?"

"Yes."

"Here," Tomasso said, shoving a package at him: some files from Personnel and three books. "There's a Bentley with a driver waiting outside. You are to deliver this to the Star Maker personally. At his office. No straying on the set, understand? This is a bad day."

"Okay," Mortimer said, taking the package.

"One minute." Tomasso bit his lip; his face clouded. "Mort, I shouldn't say this, but . . . don't let the Star Maker talk you into anything."

"Talk me into what?"

"Look at me." Tomasso hiked his trouser leg up, revealing his artificial limb. He turned his unseeing eye on Mortimer. "Do I have to spell it out for you?"

"I'll take care of myself," Mortimer said placatingly.

"Wait. You've got the hots for Polly Morgan, haven't you?"

"The hell I have."

"Well, you warn her to take care too. You warn her to take special care."

Still Mortimer failed to comprehend.

"Do not repeat this, but the Star Maker no longer rigidly believes in his own immortality. He plans to double-cross us all. He wants an heir."

"Marriage," Mortimer asked, aghast, "at his age?"

"Marriage? Go know. After all these years, go know. You'd better get moving. You're late already."

What, Mortimer wondered, speeding toward the studios, was Tomasso getting at? Surely the Star Maker was no longer capable of producing an heir. Unless the cunning old bastard had test tubes full of his semen stored away in a deep-freeze somewhere. He invites an unsuspecting, beautiful young girl, say Polly Morgan, to his suite, then when she's least expecting it, whamo! Artificial insemination. Nonsense. And yet – and yet – what did he need these three books for? *Feeding Your Baby and Child*, by Spock and Lowenberg, *Your Baby and You*, by Seymour Freed, and *Natural Childbirth*, by Grantly Dick Reid. Mortimer turned to the files he had been given. The medical history and X-ray data on three girls from the typing pool, including the replacement for poor Miss Spaight, who had died while undergoing her hysterectomy. *And Polly Morgan's case history!* Peeking, Mortimer discovered that Polly was still a virgin, of all things. How very, very odd, he thought. But what did the obscene, undying Star Maker want with these files? Was he about to select a mistress?

Mortimer climbed out of the Bentley opposite Sound Stage D, which was ringed with black-uniformed guards. As two guards closed in on him, Mortimer showed his pass and was instructed to take the first stairway to the right, which would lead him to the Star Maker's suite. But once inside the studio, Mortimer was drawn to the heavy door to the sound stage.

He had never been on a film set before. Pushing open the door, he slipped inside. The studio was enormous but stark, with the size and feel of a factory floor, heavily scaffolded, huge lights suspended from ropes. In the far corner, Mortimer made out a high-spirited, elegantly dressed group, drinking champagne and eating smoked salmon and caviar from a long table. Dominating the party, looking curiously sad and preoccupied amid such gaiety, stood the towering Star. This, Mortimer thought, must be the last-day party for the unit; he had read about such things. Stepping cautiously over open paint buckets, careful not to trip over tangled black cables, threading his way between flats, Mortimer, keeping to the shadows, gradually edged closer to the group, recognizing the faces of familiar actors and actresses.

Then, from his vantage point, Mortimer noticed something decidedly odd. Black-suited motorcycle riders moved from door to door, locking all but one. Other black-suited riders, their faces expressionless, filtered through among the celebrants, ushering them out of the unlocked door. While the riders seemed intent on emptying the studio, the Star rushed from guest to guest, imploring them to stay on, this laconic hero of a thousand cinema duels looking absolutely petrified. The Star's terror, it seemed to Mortimer, was edging on hysteria, as one by one the guests melted away. Soon there were but two performers left drinking with the Star, a well-known character actor and a gorgeous actress. An impatient black-suited rider strode up to them, whispered something, and they instantly put down their unfinished drinks.

"No, no, stay," the Star shrieked. "Have another one."

Apologetically, they retreated.

"*Please stay. Please, please.*"

As soon as they were out of the door, the bolt was driven home and the lock was secured. Then, silence. The towering Star walked up to the long table, lips curled defiantly, and poured himself a glass of champagne, just as he had done when threatened in so many films past. Only this time there was an added detail. Tears streamed down the Star's cheeks.

Mortimer, his heart thumping, watched as two black-suited men carried out a thin seven-foot-long black box and set it down on the floor with immense care. They were followed by two more men, wheeling an incredible-looking machine with a menacing pumplike device attached. The men rolled the rubber-wheeled machine to a stop beside the long black box and immediately began to adjust a number of dials. Then a studio door cracked open and shut, admitting two of the Star Maker's doctors and a very pretty, giggly nurse.

"Ready! Steady! *Go!*"

The doctors and the nurse, wearing white, raced for the long table and began to gorge themselves on champagne and caviar. They were indifferent to the black-suited riders who now began to close in on the Star.

"No," the Star howled, picking up an empty bottle, "not this time, you don't."

"Double negative," one of the doctors said to the nurse, making her fall about with laughter.

The circle of black-suited men tightened. Klieg lights were flicked on, searching out the Star.

"Now come on," the leader of the black-suited riders pleaded. "Be a good boy."

"*No!*"

"Why make trouble for us? In the end . . ."

"I'm not going to let you do it. Not this time."

"But you're going to start on another film in a month's time. Thirty-one days from today."

"That's what you promised last time. I want a life of my own. I want to get married. I –"

"Don't make me laugh."

"If you let me go," the Star begged, retreating, "I'll be good. I'll do anything you say. So help me God."

"Don't be childish. You know the rules."

Without warning, two black-suited riders lunged for the Star. He avoided them, disappearing among the flats.

"Now remember, guys, he's not to be damaged. It's as much as your life is worth if you so much as bruise him."

One of the doctors bounced the nurse on his lap. The other doctor, having had his fill of smoked salmon, began to wrap what he couldn't eat. Suddenly there came the clatter of a man pulling desperately against a locked door. A whistle blew. "There he is," one of the black-suited riders called out.

As the riders regrouped, closing in on the Star, the doctor opened his legs, letting the nurse crash to the floor. He picked up a syringe and started wearily toward the Star.

"Easy does it. Now remember, guys. You mustn't puncture him."

Once more the adroit survivor of a hundred and one cinema chases eluded his pursuers, knocking over and shattering a klieg light.

"Where is he now?"

"That's not our problem. It's the broken glass we've got to worry about."

"Christ!"

"You two. Sweep it up immediately. All we need is for him to trip over that."

Now the nurse sat on the other doctor's lap, shoveling caviar into his mouth until the cheeks were inflated.

"Over there!"

The Star was trapped in a spotlight, high over the studio floor, swinging from a cable, reminding Mortimer, more than anything else, of his Academy Award-winning *Captain Kidd's Revenge*.

"If you come a step closer," the Star shrieked girlishly, "I'll throw myself down."

"Oh, no, you wouldn't. You'll break."

"I don't care."

A black-suited rider whistled as he opened the long black

box, velvet-lined and mothproofed. The doctor with the syringe approached again, suppressing a yawn.

"Lower him down gently," the leader of the black-suited riders called out when suddenly Mortimer was seized from behind. He jumped.

"What are you doing here?" a rider demanded.

Another rider twisted Mortimer's arm high behind his back.

"I've come to see the Star Maker. I have some confidential papers with me."

"You'd better, baby. You'd better."

As Mortimer was hustled off, the Star's shrieks continued unabated, silence coming only when the heavy studio door slid shut behind him.

"You'd be Griffin, Mortimer Griffin," the Star Maker said cordially.

Wincing with pain, Mortimer nodded.

"Let him go. Griffin's got an absolutely marvy lymphatic system. Isn't that right?"

Mortimer nodded dumbly.

"Did you bring the papers and books?"

"Yes."

"Good boy! You can leave us alone now, fellas, it's perfectly all right. Pour yourself a drink, Griffin. Over there," the Star Maker said, indicating the bar.

Gratefully Mortimer helped himself to a large brandy.

The Star Maker's handsomely appointed suite was overheated, silk curtains drawn against the sunlight. The desk, the surface covered in tooled green leather, was the work of a seventeenth-century Florentine craftsman. A carved piece of Chinese jade served as a paperweight. The desk-lamp base was carved out of ivory, the work of an Ashanti tribesman. All the other furnishings, at first glance, were also rare and ruggedly masculine, except for a far corner set off by frilly blue curtains. This corner was bare except for a rug made of chinchilla skins, and a frail-looking bassinet hewn of hand-carved oak.

"It was Henry the Third's of France," the Star Maker said, and went on to explain that in deference to Henry III, who wished to be a woman, French sovereigns were referred to by the feminine gender: "*Sa majesté.*"

Mortimer had, until now, avoided looking directly at the Star Maker, who was not seated in the customary wheelchair. Instead, the old thing was lolling on a bed, under an enormous oil painting of Tiresias, on Mount Cyllene, watching two snakes coupling. Crocheted pillows were propped under the Star Maker's massive head, and a lead taped to an artery in his arm ran to a renal dialyzer, wherein the Star Maker's blood flowed over one side of a semipermeable membrane of Cuprophane, and was cleansed of undesirable molecules and toxic materials before it ran into the body through another vein. A most efficient-looking nurse attended the dialyzer. "Kidney rinse," the Star Maker said, nose crinkling. "I'll only be another minute. Won't I, dear?"

"Yes, sir."

Mortimer waited, trying not to stare, while the nurse unstrapped it. The Star Maker smiled back reassuringly and Mortimer noticed, for the first time, that now the right eye was swimming with cataracts. Then, mercifully, the nurse drew a curtain round the Star Maker and Mortimer hastened to pour himself another drink.

Soon the Star Maker emerged in a wheelchair, cheeks pink, legs tucked under a rug, the right leg dangling at least six inches lower than the left, the shoe on the right foot easily two sizes larger than the shoe on the left. "Now then," the Star Maker asked, "are you comfy?"

"Yes," Mortimer said.

"Thank you, nurse," the Star Maker said, waving the right, absolutely unwrinkled hand. The other hand was wizened. Something else Mortimer found unnerving; the Star Maker's voice tended to crack in mid-sentence, wavering between soprano and baritone.

"Only a half hour to your next injection," the nurse said, departing.

The Star Maker nodded, leaning forward for Mortimer to light a cigar. On the Star Maker's lap there were knitting needles, a ball of blue wool, and the beginnings of a baby's blue sweater. "You weren't supposed to enter the studio. It was naughty of you, Griffin. Very. How much did you see?"

Mortimer told him.

"Soon I won't have any secrets left. And do you enjoy publishing?"

"Yes. That is to say, I did until –"

"You peeked at the Our Living History file?"

"Well, now that you mention it, there is something I'd like to ask you."

"Good. Very good. You see, Dino Tomasso won't be with us much longer. He'll be going into the hospital again soon, poor devil. The other eye. Unsavable."

"Oh, my God, how awful!"

"You mustn't worry. I will always take care of Dino. He shall never want for anything." The Star Maker leaned forward in the wheelchair. "Remember this, Griffin. The revolution eats its own. Capitalism recreates itself."

Mortimer didn't comment.

"I want you to take over Oriole. The whole shebang."

"What?"

"Another drink?"

"If you don't mind?"

There was a knock at the door. A nurse entered accompanied by a black-suited rider. While the nurse injected an estrogenic preparation – actually 1 cc. of estradiol undecylate – into the Star Maker's arm, the Star Maker studied the typewritten sheet the rider had left behind. Once the nurse and rider had departed, the Star Maker, still reading, crossed arms over chest, cupping the breasts, probing gently for renewed gynecomastia. "Oh, well," the Star Maker muttered consolingly, "can't rush such a delicate thing as titties, can we?" Then the Star Maker fixed Mortimer with an icy stare. "We can trust you, can't we, Mortimer? May I call you Mortimer?"

"Yes. Now, there's the question of the Our Living History series. The file –"

"Of course we can trust you. You've got a honey of a lymph system to live up to."

"You are avoiding my –"

"Hardly. I will keep no secrets from the man who runs Oriole for me. Mortimer, do you realize that in all my years, my considerable years, you are the first man to smoke out why I am really called the Star Maker?"

"Am I?"

"What was it you said to Tomasso?" the Star Maker asked, chuckling. "'He has the emptiest face I've ever seen on the screen.' Harsh words, Mortimer."

"I'm sorry."

"Never apologize for brilliance. You could be invaluable to me, Mortimer."

"Could I?"

"Having guessed so much, Mortimer, I feel I owe it to you to tell you the story from the beginning . . . Now where to begin, where to begin. Let me put it to you this way." The Star Maker paused and took a deep breath, finally whispering the name of one of the most celebrated film stars of the 1940's who had, Mortimer recalled, died of a heart attack in 1954. "He isn't dead."

"*What?*"

"He isn't dead. He was never born. He didn't exist."

"You're making fun of me."

"No. Not at all. But you're going to have to be patient. I must begin at the true beginning," the Star Maker said, taking up the knitting again. "Let me first assure you that there are no Elders of Zion. There never was such a group."

"But it never occurred to me for a moment," Mortimer protested.

"I have never favored the conspiracy theory of history. Why, even in the Middle Ages there never were any Jewish ritual murders. It's a load of crap, Mortimer."

"I never thought otherwise."

"Good. Jews, on the other hand –"

"Are you, um, Jewish?"

"Not to begin with. That is to say, I'm Greek-born."

"I don't understand."

The Star Maker chuckled. "Well, what I'm getting at is me – these days, I'm a little bit of everything, you know. Pieces and patches." The Star Maker's smile ebbed. "Now, as I was saying, Jews, on the other hand, do tend to be influential beyond their numbers in certain selected spheres. Say, philosophy, medical science, banking, the arts . . . and, well, obviously Hollywood, the cinema arts . . . Now, going back to the thirties, the *nineteen* thirties I mean, those were the days of the colossals, the big studios, and I'm revealing nothing if I say most of these studios were owned and run by non-Americans. The foreign-born. Jews, Greeks, Italians. Now the giants are dead. I, of course, still own and run Star Maker Studios, among other ventures . . ."

Mortimer, remembering a conversation with Polly Morgan, who knew absolutely everything about the cinema, said, "In those early days, you made the Gasoline Alley films. Rather like the Andy Hardy series."

"Exactly. It was on our conscience."

"What was?"

"The WASPs. There we were, you see, a handful of kikes, dagos, and greaseballs, controlling the images Protestant America worshiped. We taught you that to be inarticulate, rather stupid in fact, like Gary Cooper, was manly. It was even manlier to avoid women. Our power was tremendous, you know. Prodigious. When Clark Gable turned up without a vest in *It Happened One Night* he practically killed the undershirt industry. We set the style in big tits. Etc., etc. But what I'm getting at is power, you know, has its responsibilities. Once a year we met to decide what we could do for the *goyim*. One year we gave them Andy Hardy and another Alice Faye or John Wayne. Anything to prop up the myths of the American heartland. . . . Well now, at the same time, to be honest, the stars we had under contract were beginning to give us trouble. This one was a queer, that one a nympho, and the next a shithead. Suddenly names we had made big – former waitresses and ditchdiggers – wanted script approval, if only to show they could read. Things were getting messy, Mortimer.

"I retreated to Las Vegas to ruminate. There was, I decided, nothing more vacuous, no shell emptier, than a movie actor. They speak the words writers put in their mouths. Any writer. If it's a woman and her legs are bad you shoot somebody else's legs for her. If she's got no tits you build her some, borrowing fat from her thighs. If she can't sing, you hire somebody to dub for her. If it's a man, somebody does his stunts for him. If he can't remember his lines you hold up an idiot card out of shot for him and do one line at a time, over and over again, maybe twenty-five times, until he gets it right. If he has no hair you stitch some on to him. If he's too short, you stretch him. You handle his women and money for him. You rewrite his past life for him. . . . Was I, the Star Maker, going to be dependent on the whims of such fleas? In a word, no.

"I returned to Hollywood and shared my thoughts with other studio heads and at long last they began to take a positive interest in my nonprofit science foundation. Mortimer, you should have seen my lab in those days! What a bunch of scientists I had! They came to me from the Vienna Radium Institute and Göttingen; from Rutherford's lab at Cambridge; from the University of Munich and Tokyo; from M.I.T. and Princeton and Breslau. The cream of the cream. I read them Edward Gordon Craig's piece on the übermarionette. I brought in von Sternberg to tell them what he thought about actors. I told them about the contract troubles we were having with the stars and how we had to suppress the squalid details of their personal lives. Gentlemen, I said, each one of you here is a genius. You can have anything you want. Now get into that lab and don't come out again until you've made me a Star."

"What?" Mortimer asked.

"Easier said than done, as you can guess. Previously only God... But then with the other studios behind me at last, with a limitless budget, we set to work in earnest. The idea was to kill two birds with one stone. By manufacturing our own stars, no more than one model to a mold, we would be liberated from our contract troubles and so forth. By making our first star the prototype goy, we would be doing something uplifting for America.

"So Operation Goy-Boy began. We were under way. But who, we first had to know, was Goy-Boy, that is to say, the ideal American male? The Motivational Research boys, the pollsters, covered America for us, and came back with twenty thousand completed forms. We fed these forms into the most advanced of computers and finally settled on three body and face possibilities. Goy-Boy I, our first man-made star, was only a partial success. He moved rather well, but had only one expression. He got his lines mixed up. All the same, we put him into a picture. First day on the set the damn thing melts under the hot lights. Before our eyes, Mortimer, eight million dollars leaked through the studio floorboards. Goodbye, Goy-Boy I.

"Goy-Boy II cost us twelve million dollars, but was an enormous improvement. Two complete expressions and memory perfect. Van Thaelman, the comic on our research team (there's one in every lab, you know), went without sleep a whole weekend just to make Goy-Boy II a cock. Why, it was the cutest little thing you ever saw. If you pulled Goy-Boy II's earlobe, it stood up just like a real one. What a bunch we had in the lab, what fun we had in those days! Anyway, the big unanswered question about Goy-Boy II was would the public warm to him? Well, Mortimer, let me assure you, without naming names, that the first picture Goy-Boy II made is still on *Variety*'s list of all-time great grossers. Another generation is learning to love him as his first picture turns up again and again on TV. We still get fan mail for him –"

"What happened?" Mortimer asked.

"What happened?" The Star Maker's head shook sadly. "For the second picture we pulled the stops out. It was going to be bigger than *Gone with the Wind*. We went on location in the desert," the Star Maker said, tears welling in the eyes, "and the second night out, my drunk of a director takes Goy-Boy II out on a binge, showing him off from bar to bar, pulling his earlobe and making his cock stand up for complete strangers. The director bought Goy-Boy II a girl, a call girl with hellishly long nails. A scratcher and a biter." The Star Maker sighed. "Goy-Boy II didn't survive his night of love. He never had a chance, poor kid. And of course we couldn't make another, because we had broken the mold.

"Which brings me to our triumph, Goy-Boy III. *The* Mini-Goy. What a piece of work! Three expressions, Mortimer. Three. Walked very, very nice. Talked in sentences as long as twelve words each. He couldn't read actual books or scripts, making him almost human, hah? But he could understand and remember synopses. Mortimer, among actors Mini-Goy passed for an intellectual. Why, women were crazy for him," the Star Maker said, slapping his knee in fond remembrance. "Anyway, we couldn't have been more thrilled. We broke open the champagne and we called him, well, you know," the Star Maker said, whispering the celebrated Star's name once more.

"You're mad, Star Maker."

The Star Maker, lost in a reverie, ignored Mortimer. "Armed with three complete expressions and sentences that ran to twelve words, no single word containing more than three syllables, he went from success to success. How were we to know there would be wear and tear, just like we mortals suffer? Here a rip. There a rub gone too deep. Somewhere else a slow leak. The Star, bless him, never said a word. Never a complaint, Mortimer. Between pictures we let the air out and locked him in a mothproof box. Maybe all that inflating and deflating? Anyway one day, I'll never forget it if I live another hundred years, one day, I was on the set. . . . In the middle of a picture, his fiftieth maybe, *bang! zam! kazoom!* He blew up. Disintegrated. Grips were wiping wet pieces of the Star off their faces. Grown men cried like babies. It was terrible, ghastly."

The Star Maker's head hung low.

"Back to the old drawing board, eh?" Mortimer ventured drunkenly, having decided to humor the old lunatic.

"Oh, there were others. We manufactured plenty of stars, some of them still going strong. But there will always be only one Mini-Goy. The others . . . well, good luck to them, but . . ."

"Who are they?"

The Star Maker grinned mischievously.

"Roy Rogers maybe?"

The Star Maker made a self-deprecating gesture, the smile noncommittal but self-satisfied.

"How did you get women to play opposite them?"

"What do you mean, how? We made them too."

"Christ Almighty!"

"Mighty, but not almighty."

"Give me some names."

"No."

"Come on, Star Maker."

"Can't."

"Susan Hayward?"

"God's, not ours," the Star Maker said, affronted.

"What about . . . um . . . Veronica Lake?"

"Flesh and blood. Would you believe it?"

"Or John Payne?"

"Now look here," the Star Maker said, "our production was small compared to His. But it was all quality stuff. This game is getting us nowhere."

"You're mad, Star Maker."

"Hah hah. After Mini-Goy exploded, we didn't throw the sponge in, you know. We continued to produce, but it wasn't the same. Our incomparable group of scientists began to break up. Some of our best geniuses went commercial. They left us for germ warfare or H-bomb production. More money for them and security, but gone forever were the joys of craftsmanship. After all, one H-bomb is very much like another, isn't it?" the Star Maker asked with a sneer. "Then Hollywood profits shriveled. We no longer had the same kind of money available for research and development. So we had to settle for TV-size models; our most successful TV Goy-Boy so far being the one in the doctor series. He comes in two versions, black-and-white and colored."

There was a knock at the door and two black-suited riders wheeled in a luncheon tray. Champagne, smoked eel, rump steak and French fried potatoes for Mortimer. Assorted pills and a glass of warm milk for the Star Maker. Afterwards, the nurse came to administer another injection.

"What is it this time, child? Hormones or iron?"

Both. Following the champagne and still more brandies, Mortimer found himself rambling on drunkenly. Confiding in a stranger. A mad stranger.

"It's been troubling you for years," the Star Maker asked, tongue clacking incredulously, "is that what you say?"

"Well, Star Maker, how would you like it if you were already convinced you had a small one, and then one day you couldn't even get *that* up any more?"

"Yes, yes. I understand. I suppose every young man likes to think he is a stud, as they say."

"Yes."

"But, my dear boy, do tell me more. You say it's small . . . but which one do you mean?"

"*Which one?*"

"Oh. Oh, I see."

"WHICH ONE?" Mortimer howled, knocking back his chair.

"You only have one, then?"

"Yes. That's right."

"Well, then. That is serious. That could be quite a handicap, my boy."

Hours later, it seemed, Mortimer looked up from under heavy lids to hear a swaying Star Maker say, "So I simply must have an heir. A son."

"A son! At your age?"

"Yes."

Mortimer laughed out loud. "You're not contemplating marriage, you obscene old bastard."

"Dear me, no."

"That's something."

"I'm told," the Star Maker said, "that Polly Morgan looks up to you."

"Really," Mortimer said, rather pleased.

"I have been given to understand that you are the one man at Oriole whom she respects."

"*What do you want with her?*"

"Easy, now. I'm a very rare blood type. Miss Morgan is the same type."

"And so?"

"In the coming months it seems likely I'm going to need the occasional pint."

"Star Maker, I'm unwell. Too much to drink. I've had enough for one day."

"You may be excused, then."

"We still haven't gone into the question of the Our Living History series."

"Mortimer, I was as shocked as you were to see the file. Tomasso certainly overreached himself there."

"Overreached? He's a murderer!"

"If that's the case, he must answer for it."

"What about the efficiency team from Frankfort?"

"Dismiss them, if you like."

"Do you expect me to believe you had no idea what was going on?"

"As you well know, I've been in and out of hospitals for months. There are so many other companies to look after . . . When you take over, Mortimer, you can have a free hand. Terminate the Our Living History series, if you like."

"I haven't said that I was willing to take over. I want to think about it."

"Then we must talk again soon. Very soon. You are now a party to more than one of my secrets, Mortimer."

"We can talk again after the holidays."

"Yes. Certainly. Meanwhile, however, you must promise not to say a word about what you saw in the studio."

"I'm not sure what I saw in the studio. I think I'm going out of my mind."

"There, there now. Promise?"

Anything to get away. "Yes," Mortimer said.

Mortimer returned to his office at Oriole just in time to find a swollen-eyed Miss Fishman cleaning out her desk.

"What's going on?"

"After all I've suffered, I will not work for a Jew-baiter. Not for one minute more."

"But my dear Miss Fishman –"

"How you must have hated me all these years."

"That's not true. On the contrary. I –"

"You will find," Miss Fishman said, gathering her things together, "that I'm not the only one here with contempt for you now. There isn't anybody at Oriole who hasn't heard about the dreadful things you've been saying to that poor Mr. Shalinsky." She left, slamming the door.

Mortimer dialed the typewriter pool and asked for a new secretary to be sent up.

"Right away, Mr. Griffin."

The new secretary was refreshingly young and pretty. Deeply suntanned as well. "My name is Gail," she said sweetly.

"Why, you're an American."

"Yes. I hope you don't mind."

"On the contrary."

Twenty-Three

NEW YEAR'S EVE.

Joyce was wriggling into her black silk evening gown, her slender arms upraised, when Mortimer was all but struck in the face with shattering, proof positive of her infidelity: big clumps of black hair, glistening with sweat, protruded from under her armpits. Ziggy had once told him, "I don't dig the *Playboy* bit, the non-touchable, cosmetic brand of pussy, if you know what I mean. I like my chicks earthy."

What a fool I've been, Mortimer thought. I should have guessed. Ziggy had only been with them for four days before he had noticed the sour lingering smell in their bedroom. Joyce didn't bring out her deodorant spray, which should have alerted him. Two more days passed before Mortimer realized that he no longer had to wait for his turn in the bathroom before breakfast. Joyce, apparently, no longer bathed first thing in the morning. Most likely, he thought, she now had her bath while he was at work. Or did she? For getting into bed that night the unthinkable had occurred to him: Joyce stinks. *Impossible.* No, no. It must be me, he had thought. The truth is I'm resentful of her because of my own inadequacy. For though neither of them mentioned it, Mortimer had not attempted to make love to Joyce since that humiliating night.

"Not pouring yourself another drink already," Joyce said.

"What if I am?"

"The evening's hardly begun."

So there it is, he thought, watching Joyce get ready for Lord Woodcock's annual New Year's Eve party. Yesterday impotent, today a cuckold. Well, he had to laugh. It was funny, really funny: he couldn't help but feel sorry for Joyce. Fastidious, hygienic Joyce. The very thought of her sliding between the sheets with hirsute, putrescent Ziggy sent him into transports of laughter. Imagine, he thought, that lotioned manicured hand slipping down toward his genital area, discovering the moldy underwear, Ziggy crawling with crabs and high as an overripe Camembert.

"What's so funny, *darling?* Tell me and I'll laugh too."

Before they've done it, Mortimer thought, reaching for his drink, maybe she rouses him by licking his big crooked toes clean of jam.

"Mortimer, are you laughing at me?"

Later, in stolen moments, tender moments, she squeezes the blackheads out of his greasy forehead. Torture, he thought. Why's she having it off with him, then? Self-punishment? No. Because he's got a big one, a fat Jewy one, a voice came back.

"Mortimer, answer me."

"You wouldn't understand," he said, staring.

"Is there anything wrong with my dress?"

"No. I'm just surprised you got into it without having a bath first."

"Perhaps I no longer suffer from the need for self-purification rituals."

Mortimer sniffed the bedroom air delicately.

"What is it now?"

"Must be a kitchen odor that's drifted up through the floorboards," he said, picking up the spray. "Surprised you haven't noticed."

"Are you, now? Well, I'm surprised you haven't noticed something else."

"Namely?"

"Our phone's being tapped."

Mortimer laughed in her face. "I can assure you," he said, "the Government is not worried about the Anti-Apartheid League. Or your nuclear disarmament activities. Much as it would please you if they were."

"Then why are there two men sitting in a car outside all day watching our house?"

"Possibly," he said, amused, "they're from the narcotics squad."

"Oh, you," Joyce said, escaping to the bathroom, slamming the door indignantly behind her.

"Ready to make the scene, my dears?" Ziggy called up.

No, Mortimer thought, not me. For he knew that everyone but Gail, delicious creature, would shun him at the party. Mortimer Griffin, the pariah of Oriole House. The Adolf Eichmann of Publishers' Row.

Following Miss Fishman's departure from his office, hardly anyone at Oriole House spoke to him, unless their purpose was to insult.

"Haven't seen you around much lately," Mortimer said to Hy one day.

"I've been combing the streets for Gentile babies," Hy replied, slipping into his Chaym ben Yussel shuffle. "We need them for our blood rituals, don't you know?"

Nobody but Gail, ubiquitous Gail, sat with him during coffee breaks or joined him for lunch at The Eight Bells. Then somebody, most likely Shalinsky himself, had fed an unspeakable item to *Private Eye*.

> How much longer will Oriole House put up with that Jew-baiting boozer of a colonial editor who recently called the gentle Jacob Shalinsky, well-known Soho character and editor of *Jewish Thought*, "a meddling Jew"?

The following day Mortimer was stopped in the street by an earnest young man who identified himself as one of Colin Jordan's lieutenants in the British Nazi Party. "We are standing by," he said. "If there's anything we can do –"

Mortimer shoved him aside. It was, however, only the beginning. To his horror, he discovered he was now on the mailing list of more than one lunatic fringe group. The Sons of Poland, the Royal Hungarian Society, Fighters for a Free Ukraine, and other groups and unaffiliated persons long alert to the international Jewish conspiracy wrote with invitations to lecture and offers of help. All of which spurred Mortimer on to heavier drinking.

Fortunately Doug, who was on holiday now, was a comfort to him. His son, it seemed, could hardly wait for Mortimer to come home from the office and take him out. Indeed, some days he waited for Mortimer outside the house.

"Let's go to a flick, Dad."

"Shouldn't I go in first and say hello to your mother?"

"Oh, she's out demonstrating."

"What about –"

"Ziggy's been out all day. Come on. Let's go."

There were even days, curiously gratifying days, when Doug was so impatient to see him that he came to collect him at Oriole House. "I told Mom you were taking me out to dinner. Just the two of us, Dad."

And now, Mortimer thought, pouring himself another drink, there was the New Year's Eve party. Old friends would turn their backs on him. Lord Woodcock, surely, would wish to speak to him about the rumors.

"Coming," Mortimer said, reconciled. "Coming."

Champagne cost a shilling a glass at Lord Woodcock's party and caviar sixpence a plate, proceeds for the wives and children of former German concentration camp guards, innocent bystanders otherwise entirely dependent on inadequate West German Government pensions.

Mortimer, avoided by the others, just as he had expected, watched as one by one guests came up to congratulate the saintly Lord Woodcock, who only last week had won another medal, the Grand Cross of the German Order of Merit, which had been presented to him on the playing fields of Dachau.

Dino Tomasso, his good eye glassy, his champagne glass spilling over, drove Mortimer into a corner. "If I were you," he said, "I wouldn't say anything here to upset the Star Maker. He wants to speak to you again, Morty, soonest."

A group of unabashed admirers collected around Dig Jones, Daphne Humber-Guest among them. Another pair of star-crossed lovers, Mortimer thought, touched. Dig and Daphne could hardly keep their hands off each other. Even now, she stood directly behind him, screwing her breasts into his back, but the sad truth was their affair had yet to be consummated. Dig and Daphne's respective agents had not yet come together on terms.

Mortimer searched everywhere for Polly, ignoring gibes about himself and Shalinsky, but nobody had seen her. Ziggy brought Mortimer a fresh drink. "Things just happen," he said, his smile aching with concern. "Life is meaningless. Totally absurd."

"Is it?"

"In the long run, we'll all be dead, you know."

An instant later Mortimer noticed Ziggy thick in a corner with Dig Jones, whispering. Again and again Dig, who was planning a new series, a different type of series, scrutinized Mortimer, sizing him up it seemed, as Ziggy talked on and on. Finally, Dig said, "I'll have to think about it, Ziggy."

"But I've seen his army documents. I've had photostats made."

"I can't promise anything."

Lord Woodcock beckoned Mortimer to his side. "I would like to speak to you," he said, "about your 'Reading for Pleasure' lectures."

"I'm sure you would," Mortimer said stiffly.

"This isn't the time or the place, but we must get together soon."

The clock struck twelve and Lord Woodcock, seeing everyone's glasses being raised for a toast, beamed and bowed. "You're too kind," he said. "This is too much. Thank you. Thank you."

Retreating, Mortimer collided with Rachel Coleman.

"They always have at least one nigger to a party," Rachel said, thrusting a brown leg between his, rubbing.

Joyce, Mortimer was pleased to notice, was watching them surreptitiously.

"Hey!" Mortimer, to his astonishment, felt a spark, a tiny hopeful spark, of excitement. "Hey, there!"

Mortimer could not recall how he had managed it, but suddenly there they were, he and Rachel, stuffing their tongues into each other's mouths, licking, biting, in the back seat of a taxi. As the taxi rocked to a stop before her flat, Mortimer wiped his hand on his trousers before he fished out money to pay the driver.

"This way," Rachel said. "Oops. Careful. There's a step there."

If Mortimer, elated but fearful, was no longer sure how he had managed to slip away from the party with Rachel, he didn't doubt why. Not for a minute. Mortimer's motives were double-pronged, if only he – if only he –

Unable to manage even a bladder-filled morning erection since that humiliating night, he had pounced on a copy of *Human Sexual Response*, hoping to have certain questions resolved for him at last. It was a marvelous book, and one could only be grateful to those more than 600 subjects who had so selflessly undergone more than 10,000 complete cycles of sexual response while the color cameras whirred. A daily orgasm for everyone from eighteen to eighty (regardless of race, color or creed) was, Mortimer agreed with the authors, an ideal well worth striving for. But, he couldn't help speculating, but would Drs. Masters and Johnson classify his ejaculations as "mere seepage"? In my dotage already, he feared. Not that this was the only question. It was one of many. For the problem inherent in such an all-embracing study (one that measured the electrocardiographic delights of manual and mechanical manipulation, natural coition with the female partner in supine, superior, or knee-chest positions and, for many female study subjects, artificial coition in supine and knee-chest positions, as well as the joys to be had from a plastic dildo) was that it asked more questions than it answered.

Mortimer, for instance, found the workings of the plastic dildo especially instructive, even illuminating. "The equipment," he read, "can be adjusted for physical variations in size, weight, and vaginal development. The rate and depth of penile thrust is initiated and controlled completely by the responding individual. As tension elevates, rapidity and depth of thrust are increased voluntarily, paralleling subjective demand. The equipment is electrically powered." Turning to another page, he learned that this electrically powered do-it-yourself prick gave women more satisfaction than anything else going. "Understandably, the maximum physiological intensity of orgasmic response subjectively reported or objectively recorded has been achieved by self-regulated mechanical or automanipulative devices." Maybe so, Mortimer allowed grudgingly, but he craved more information about the powered plastic dildo. Was it circumcized? Or black maybe? Conversely, were there attachments and coloring kits, such as went with a Mixmaster or a Black & Decker home drill? Could a female study subject unscrew the circumcized knob from the dildo and replace it with a goyishe knob? Or could she spray the dildo black or even Chinese yellow, if she fancied? Finally, if all these permutations were possible, which knob and color combo was the biggest hit?

Human Sexual Response bitterly disappointed Mortimer in failing to answer yet another question, the one which troubled him most deeply. How big was big? How small, small? What he had hoped for was comparative charts, rather like those in doctors' waiting rooms or insurance company pamphlets, which gave the recommended weight as set against a man's body shape, years, and height. What he had wanted was a penile chart which would give average limp length and expansion when stiff, as set against age, height, and race. Yes, race. For surely it was the empirical business of objective liberal scientists to confirm or demolish once and for all the myth (or fact) that Jewish cocks were thicker, Negro ones longer.

Rachel Coleman, Mortimer had reflected, putting down the book, could tell him at a glance. Rachel, he had sensed, had a vast knowledge of pricks. And so, at the New Year's Eve party when Mortimer felt that upspringing between his legs, once so familiar, now rare, he immediately decided to chance it with Rachel, his purpose two-pronged. He would, hopefully, prove to himself that his impotence was limited to his relationship with Joyce and he would inquire point-blank how she would grade him for size. Probably, he thought, if please God I can get it up, I will not even have to ask. Her reactions will suffice. If (O happy, blessed day) she takes one peek and retreats against the wall Fanny Hill fashion, muttering about my monstrous machine, this incomparably fierce engine, etc., etc., then I will know that I am, *pace* Harold Robbins, very well endowed. But if, if more likely, she yawns (would she dare laugh in my face?) and suggests other games, anything but straightforward penile penetration, then I will know, as I have feared all these years, that I am puny indeed.

Rationalizing, he decided in advance, excusing himself through loss of foreskin by circumcision, was out. Such loss, he knew, was minimal. I want the truth, he thought, as he followed after Rachel's swinging bottom into the living room . . .

the upspringing between his legs escalating beyond mere excitement, above the plateau, to a veritable throbbing and, alas, seepage. *Watch it. Don't lose it.*

"Would you care for a drink?" Rachel asked.

Mortimer pulled her to him on the sofa, his hands flying up her skirt. Rachel broke free, laughing. "Aren't you going to say sweet, flattering things to me first," she asked, her eyes taunting, "like you would to a white girl?"

To a white girl. Could it be, Mortimer thought, terrified, that this precious erection of his was impure, not sexually motivated, but politically inspired? Was it possible that the throb-throb-throb was not, as he desperately hoped, his virility returned, but only a lousy liberal gesture? The stiffening no more than white condescension? No, no. Even as he began to wilt, he looked up to see Rachel unzip and wriggle out of her skirt to stand before him in her deliciously diaphanous underthings. She put on a record, Satchmo at Carnegie Hall, and handed him a drink. "Cheers," she said, lifting him to his feet.

"Cheers." Up up up. Thank God, he thought, dancing with her, his hands squeezing her bottom.

"You have no idea what a sexy chap you are, Mortimer."

"We can talk later," he said, struggling with the straps of her bra.

Once more her expression was scornful. "Nothing works you guys up like coon music, does it?"

"Now look here."

"You look here," she said, coolly opening a side-table drawer and bringing out a pen and a blank check. "What's your bank, baby?"

"Lloyd's. Why?"

"Branch?"

He told her. Thrusting against him, rubbing, she handed him a check made out for twenty-five pounds. "Sign this first."

"What the hell for?"

"Because this world being imperfect, this world being what it is, no ofay is capable of balling with a black girl without paying for it."

"That's not true."

"You'd feel guilty in the morning."

"You're too touchy, Rachel."

"Sign, baby."

"But it runs counter to my political principles. It's not the money –"

"Good," she said, thrusting the pen and check at him.

"– but –"

Rachel smiled lasciviously at him, running her tongue over her lips, squeezing her breasts, rotating her pelvis.

"Why, you're nothing but a whore!"

"Didn't I tell you?" she said, satisfied. "In the end, you're all the same. You feel your racial superiority is being compromised if you hump a poor little, uninhibited colored girl without paying for it."

Still, he hesitated.

"Don't you see, honey? I'm taking the bread for your sake."

"All right, then," Mortimer said, signing. "But you're going to earn it, see?"

"Didn't I know it? Didn't I call the shot? Underneath, you're all bigoted."

"Look here, Rachel –"

"This," she said, blowing on the signature, "doesn't cover specialties. The bigger the guilt, baby, the higher the cost."

"I do not go in for . . . specialties. It's information I'm after. I'm going to want your objective opinion on a couple of things. About me, um, in comparison to other men. I'll show you what I mean in a minute," he said, unbuttoning his shirt.

"But I can already tell you something about little old you. I keep my ears open. Dino Tomasso's not going to be with us much longer –"

Too true, Mortimer remembered, briefly sad.

"– and you're number-one candidate for his job, white boy. Hy Rosen hasn't a hope."

Inexplicably, the anger rose in him. "Incidentally, how much did Hy make out *his* check for?"

"Rosen? Don't think he didn't try, but this pussy doesn't cream for Jew boys."

Migod.

"Which reminds me," she said, "I hope it isn't true what Jake Shalinsky says."

"*What does Jake Shalinsky say?*"

"That secretly you're a Yid yourself."

"The hell I am. What ever made you even suspect –"

"Well, Jews often change their names, don't they? They try and pass, the worst of them. But in the buff, there's no mistaking a Jew man, is there, honey?" Laughing, Rachel pulled him to her. "Come on. We're wasting time."

But Mortimer, his trousers lying in a pool at his ankles, hastily whipped them up again.

"What's the matter?"

"Nothing." But he ripped a nail zipping up his fly.

"Baby," she said, coyly covering her bosom with one hand and lowering another between her legs, "I'm getting a chill, just standing here."

"Get me another drink, you filthy black whore."

"Yassah, boss. Right away, massah."

She returned to find him dressed.

"You going?"

"That's right, Beulah. Good night."

Twenty-Four

MORTIMER LET THE PHONE ring. Ring and ring. Finally somebody answered.

"*Jewish Thought* here."

"Shalinsky?"

"Mr. Shalinsky is in Manchester. I'll have him get in touch with your office the minute he returns."

"Shalinsky, it's you."

"Ah, it's you, Griffin. Happy New Year, as they say."

"The same to you."

"Sorry. I thought it was Levitt the printer. He's the only one who ever phones me so early in the morning. *Wei geht's?*"

"Pardon?"

"How are you?"

"Oh, fine. *Just fine.* Look here, Shalinsky, I've got some papers I'd like to show you."

"Good."

Taken aback, Mortimer said, "What do you mean, good?"

"I was hoping you'd want to talk."

"Can I come over now? Right now?"

"Absolutely."

It was seven thirty in the morning, New Year's Day. An hour earlier, Mortimer, his head throbbing, his step uncertain, the drink rising in his stomach, had slipped into his own house while everyone was still asleep, and gathered the necessary papers together.

Mortimer had amassed all manner of personal documents. His birth certificate, his passport, marriage license, University of Toronto graduation certificate, a Rotary Club public speaking award, his unemployment insurance card, vaccination certificate, Bo-lo Champion (Junior Division) Award of Merit, three library cards, a parking ticket and his Barclaycard. On all these documents was the name Mortimer Lucas Griffin. Seething with suppressed anger, he watched as Shalinsky fingered each document pensively. At last Shalinsky looked up, pinching his lower lip between thumb and index finger. "Facts," he said. "Documents. So what?"

"So what? God damn it, Shalinsky, you must stop going around telling people that I'm a Jew. All this goes to prove that I was born a white Anglo-Saxon Protestant named Mortimer Lucas Griffin."

"To think that you would go to so much trouble. What are you afraid of, Griffin?"

"Afraid? Me!"

"Am I a chatterbox?"

"Yes. But there's nothing to chatter about. Are you mad, Shalinsky?"

"I'm not mad. Neither do I wish to make problems for you. We should stick together, Griffin."

"What do I have to do to prove to you that I'm not Jewish?"

Shalinsky began to sift through Mortimer's papers again, as if to soothe a bad-tempered child. "And what about your father?" he asked. "Couldn't he have changed your name without your knowing it?"

"Or my grandfather. What about him?"

"You're so excited."

"You're ruining my life, Shalinsky."

"Mr. Griffin, please. I hardly know you."

"Look here, Shalinsky, do you think *everyone* is Jewish?"

"Certainly not," he said, offended.

"Well, that's something. There are lots of people, you know, upstanding types, who just happen to have been born Gentiles. Like me."

"Mediocrities, the lot."

"Oh, my God, Shalinsky."

"Isn't it a proven fact, Griffin, that most of the world's great men are Jews?"

"Like hell it is."

"Take your own age, *par exemple*. This age of angst," Shalinsky said, lowering his eyes. "Sigmund Freud, he was a pork eater, I suppose. Karl Marx, *alavah sholem*. Well? There you have it, Griffin. The two greatest influences on the twentieth century."

"And what about Stalin?"

"Trotsky had more bloody brains in his little finger than –"

"That's not the point. Stalin triumphed and he was a Gentile, wasn't he? A priest."

"His wife wore the pants."

"I have no interest in stale Kremlin gossip."

"Her maiden name was Epstein."

"What am I going to do with you, Shalinsky?"

"You want to be one of them? I don't understand you, Griffin." Shalinsky stood up. "*They killed Marilyn Monroe.*" Then, as an afterthought, he added, "One of ours by choice. By choice, *chaver*."

"Give me Ingrid Bergman any time."

"Beautiful women you want to talk about? Elizabeth Taylor, there's another acquisition to our faith."

"And what about . . . Audrey Hepburn?"

"That one, with her little boy's body? Mr. Griffin, please. Among us we like something – well, that you can get your teeth into."

"Oh, what's the use!"

"Literature you're worried about. Kafka. Proust. Pasternak. Herman Wouk."

"Tolstoy!"

"It's the exception that makes the rule. There are rumors and reports, mind you. I. M. Sinclair has a theory –"

"André Gide. I suppose he was a rabbi's son."

Shalinsky was indignant. "Gide was a pederast," he said. "Among them, you know."

"Just what do you mean, 'among them'? Are there no Jewish queers?"

"Mr. Griffin, I thought this was a serious discussion. An exchange of ideas."

"Never mind, skip it."

"And furthermore did you know that behind the discovery of America there was a Jewish financier?"

"Oh, that wouldn't surprise me for a minute."

"Luis de Santangel. And with Columbus there sailed at least three Jews. The ship's surgeon, the interpreter and the map maker, Abraham Zacuto."

"Sure. All the soft jobs . . . Shalinsky, this is getting us nowhere. The fact is I'm not Jewish, as these documents plainly show."

"One thing," Shalinsky said, after a long pause. "Among all these documents, no army discharge papers. Why, I ask myself."

In a flash, Mortimer gathered up his papers and was gone. Outside, he was gratified to find a taxi waiting.

"Where to, guv?" Dr. Laughton asked in his best Cockney.

Mortimer gave him his home address and leaned back, his eyes shut.

Twenty-Five

IT WAS ALMOST NINE IN the morning when Mortimer returned wearily to his house and found Doug eating corn flakes in the kitchen.

"Happy New Year, Doug," Mortimer said warmly.

"Same to you, Dad."

Mortimer ran his hand through his son's hair. He managed a grin. "I'm bushed. Would you excuse me if I didn't join you and went right to sleep?"

"Oh, I wouldn't go in there, Dad. You'd be on a sticky wicket, rather."

"How come?"

"Uncle Ziggy's in bed with her."

"*In our bedroom?*"

"Just so."

"Oh, you poor kid, when did you find out about them?"

"Why, I've known from the beginning. Mother told me everything."

"Everything? You mean about my, um, illness too?"

Doug lowered his eyes. Mortimer found the brandy and poured himself a stiff one. "Did she have to tell you that?" he asked, tears in his eyes.

"Don't cry. She explained it wasn't hereditary. She said I needn't worry, actually."

"How could she?" he said, sinking into a chair.

"It wasn't exactly her fault. She didn't want to tell me. But I couldn't help noticing how cross she's been . . . and, well, how absolutely super she's felt since Uncle Ziggy's come to stay with us."

"Good old Ziggy."

"Naturally they wanted me out most afternoons and Mother wasn't going to be dodgy with me about that. I couldn't respect her any more if she wasn't completely honest with me."

"I see."

"It could have given me a trauma."

"Your mother is so considerate."

"I don't blame her. Do you? I've read that women need it rather more as they grow old and wrinkly while chaps pass their peak early."

"I have never slapped your face, Doug. But if you don't stop –"

"But Mother says you've got a colored bird. I don't understand, Dad, if you can have a go with a black one, why can't –"

"Shettup!"

Which was when Ziggy stumbled into the kitchen, scratching his groin. Mortimer's dressing gown was too big for him.

"Hi," Mortimer said, "old pal."

"A *guten yor*. How'd you make out with your *Schwartze?*"

"I do not wish to discuss such matters before my son."

"Aw, come on. You're not pissed off, are you?"

"Oh, no. I'm immensely pleased for the two of you."

"I always stick up for you with her, you know."

"Thanks."

"Aw."

"Joyce will be more precious to me now that you've found her attractive. I always thought she bored you."

"I told her if we're going to have a thing, it's got to be above board. You had to know."

"And what did my adorable wife say to that?"

"She's very put out with you, baby. Over Rachel Coleman. And this –"

"I'm not having an affair with Rachel Coleman."

"– Shalinsky business. Mortimer, tell me something. Do Jews make you feel inferior?"

"Certainly not!"

"No kidding?" Ziggy scratched his head, impressed. "You know there are times when I think she's using me only to get at you."

"Maybe we shouldn't talk so loud. I'd hate to wake her up, the whore."

"Please don't be messy, Dad."

"What would *you* like me to do, Doug?"

"I think you should cut out for a while and let them be. I'll come and stay with you on weekends, if you like. Maybe you could take me to Paris next weekend?"

"Do either of you mind if I have a word with Joyce?"

"Be dignified, Dad."

"I don't mind," Ziggy said, "but the kid's right. This isn't a good time. Not after the way you came on at the party."

"What?"

"Man, you practically raped that Rachel Coleman chick on the sofa."

"If it's no inconvenience," Mortimer said, grabbing his coat, "I'll send for my things later today."

"*Ciao.*"

"*Ciao.*"

Twenty-Six

Lord Woodcock phoned again and again, a black-suited motorcycle rider from the Star Maker went round twice, but Mortimer, settled in at the Prince Albert Hotel on Cromwell Road, continued to feign illness. Drinking himself to sleep at night, he imagined they did it together on the floor. Or in the bathtub. Bed would be too conventional for Ziggy.

Together, he thought, they're having a good laugh at me.

"Do you know what," Joyce tells him, giggling, "Mortimer has insurance."

"What a square," Ziggy says, marveling.

"He's also got money in a building society. Put away against a rainy day," Joyce says, nudging him.

"Is it, ah, a joint account? Can you make withdrawals too?"

"Yes. Once the income tax made a mistake in his favor and do you know what? He wrote them, enclosing a check."

"Stop. You're kidding me."

"Did you notice the seat belts?"

"In the car? Yeah."

"Wait, this is the best, Ziggy, he never flies anywhere without making a will and leaving it in a sealed envelope for me."

"Crazy."

Crazy. *I'm* crazy, Mortimer thought. I should charge into the bedroom with a knife and cut them both down. The stink, migod, every time she raises her arms, those black maggoty clumps. I should –

But when he visited, he was controlled, subdued, even with Ziggy.

"Life is totally absurd," Ziggy once said. "Like who ever would have thought you'd be visiting me here? Oh, I left all the bills and stuff on the hall table for you."

"Thanks."

"She wants to have my child, a son by Ziggy, but I put my foot down there, Mortimer."

"Good for you."

"Like it would be terrible to be my son. The kids born of famous artists are always zeros."

I should charge him with a knife, Mortimer thought, but there's my son to consider. My no longer misguided son, he reminded himself, extracting pleasure from this, his one small triumph.

To begin with, Mortimer had feared for Miss Ryerson, for after only two days at Beatrice Webb House, she had looked a wreck. By the end of the week her eyes were red and puffy and she was willing to throw the sponge in. Then, within a fortnight, the metamorphosis took place. On a day when Mortimer happened to be visiting the house, come to collect more clothes, Doug came home from school, his eyes shining, his manner quiescent. "Good afternoon, sir," he said to Mortimer.

Sir.

Then, excusing himself, he went to his room to do his prep.

"Prep?" Mortimer asked Joyce, astonished. "At Beatrice Webb House?"

Yes, Joyce confessed unhappily, and not only that. Doug had asked the news agent to cancel his subscription to *Playboy* and send him *Knowledge* magazine instead.

Finally Doug emerged from his room, politely asking for a glass of milk and a peanut butter sandwich.

"How are things at school these days?" Mortimer asked.

"Absolutely super! Miss Ryerson makes you feel so good."

"Really!"

"Now, if you'll excuse me, sir, I must get back to work."

"One minute, Doug."

"Yes, sir."

"Mustn't overdo the studies, eh?"

"But Ryerson doesn't like it if you don't do well. If you do well she makes you feel good all over."

"All right. Off you go, then," Mortimer said, beaming at Joyce.

"Mortimer, there's something I should –"

"William Golding is all wet. Kids, you see, are basically good. Given strong moral leadership –"

"– say to you."

"About you and Ziggy?"

"Yes."

"I'm not interested. He's going to walk out on you, you know. If not this month, next. But I'm not taking you back."

"Ziggy has made me aware of my womanhood for the first time. It's like taking LSD. A whole new sensual world has been opened to me."

"Spare me the details, please."

"After we've made love," she said breathlessly, "he doesn't wash."

After, before, Mortimer thought.

"Because when he's alone," she continued, "creating, well . . ." Joyce paused to smooth out her skirt. "It inspires him to be able to have me on his fingertips, if you get my meaning."

"Yes, I do, alas."

"Now, you'd never think of that."

"It's poetry."

"Yes. I think so."

"And so natural," he added snidely.

"Oh, you, you're so inhibited." All at once, Joyce's face filled with concern. "Mortimer, are you any . . . better?"

Get stuffed, he thought, gulping down his drink.

"Perhaps you should see an analyst?"

"There's something I want out of the bedroom, if you don't mind?"

"Go right ahead."

Mortimer avoided looking at the unmade bed. He dug right into the bottom drawer of the dresser and pulled out the strongbox with the combination lock. His army documents. The medal. At least she and Ziggy would not have this to mock.

Safe in his hotel room again, Mortimer poured himself a brandy, unlocked the strongbox and, for the first time in years, confronted his war trophy, his throat tightening. The phone rang, startling him, the ringing reaching out of the terrifying past, making his hands shake.

Dig Jones again. No, Mortimer said, he appreciated the higher offer, but money wasn't the issue. He wasn't interested in appearing on Dig's new show.

"What did he say?" Ziggy asked.

"He said no."

"Shit."

"Not to worry," Dig said. "He'll come round."

"How can you be so sure?"

Once more Dig fingered the photostats Ziggy had brought him. "Because I haven't made my best offer yet."

"Money won't tempt him. Like he isn't hip, you know."

"Not to worry, man."

Twenty-Seven

"I HAVE ASKED YOU to be present for this little discussion," Dr. Booker said, "because it was you, after all, who recommended Miss Ryerson to us."

"Doug tells me," Mortimer said, hard put to conceal his complacency as he beamed at Miss Ryerson, "that you made him feel good all over."

"And how is Doug?" Miss Ryerson asked. "Not neglecting his prep, I hope?"

"Hardly."

"Miss Ryerson's boys," Dr. Booker interrupted, "are most devoted to her."

"That doesn't astonish me." Mortimer smiled, graciously, he hoped, for he had not come to gloat.

"They say grace at her table. In the Beatrice Webb dining hall."

"Well, Dr. Booker," Mortimer said, with a quick wink for Miss Ryerson, "there are worse offenses, aren't there?"

"So you don't know?"

"Know what, Dr. Booker?"

"Fuss and bother," Miss Ryerson said.

"Miss Ryerson has been *grading* the boys in the second form."

"Well, marks in themselves –"

"Do you know why?"

"Obviously to separate –"

"The men from the boys? She has been grading them. She has been giving them . . . exams. Oral exams. Written exams. Each fortnight, Mr. Griffin, she informs the boys of their rank in class."

"So what?"

"Ranks one, two, three, and four are then separated from the rest of the class. The rest of the class is dismissed and ranks one, two, three and four stay behind. They stay behind for a special treat. Is that correct, Miss Ryerson?"

"So far."

"Would you come to the point, please?"

"She blows them, Mr. Griffin."

"*What?*"

"You heard me."

Mortimer turned to Miss Ryerson. "I don't believe a word of it," he said emphatically.

"Blowing?" Miss Ryerson looked baffled. "Is that a slang expression, Mortimer?"

Mortimer nodded, his cheeks flaring red, and he looked at the floor.

"Oh, I understand," Miss Ryerson said. "Now I know what Dr. Booker means. But of course it's true."

"Ranks one, two, three, and four," Dr. Booker said, glaring at Mortimer.

"Shoot. It's worked wonders. Why ever are you so upset, Dr. Booker?"

"Do you realize what would happen if this leaked out?"

"Let's all try to remain calm," Mortimer said.

"I've put years into making this school what it is. Groups come from all over Europe –"

"Mortimer, my first week at Beatrice Webb House was a revelation to me. I swear I never set eyes on such a band of hooligans before."

"– from all over Europe to study our pioneering techniques. And now this."

"Not only were the boys totally deficient in Christian manners," Miss Ryerson said, "but they couldn't spell or do sums."

"One minute," Mortimer pleaded. "Do I understand this right, Miss Ryerson? You mean you actually –"

"Yes," Dr. Booker said. "And I know what you're thinking."

"Do you?"

"Maybe this in itself is not reactionary. After all, the experience, considered in isolation, can be beautiful, don't you agree?"

Mortimer hesitated.

"Come on, Griffin. Man to man."

"Okay, okay."

"But have you any idea where it leads? Inevitably?"

"Well, I –"

"Exactly. One day she rewards ranks one, two, three, and four with blow jobs, the next she starts handing out . . . *distinction cards*. Or, God help us, *good conduct badges*."

"Mortimer," Miss Ryerson interrupted, "when I first came here the boys in the second form hardly knew which end of a book was which. And filthy; I've never heard such language."

"Yes, Miss Ryerson."

"Don't you see, Griffin? It looks progressive, but what it amounts to is backsliding. Wham. We're back in the Middle Ages. We've reintroduced the reward system. Soul-destroying, capitalist-style competition. *Rivalry*, Mr. Griffin."

"You needn't raise your voice so," Miss Ryerson said.

"Do you realize what a lad suddenly demoted to number five feels? Let me tell you. When he's asked to leave early on Friday afternoon with the rest of the losers, he actually experiences physical pain. Griffin, have you ever been inside one of those old-fashioned, establishmentarian schools, where –"

"As a matter of fact, Dr. Booker, he graduated from one. Didn't you, Mortimer?"

"Yes, Miss Ryerson."

"– where children are asked to memorize? Reactionary historical dates and multiplication tables. Where they win prizes or cups for conformist-style achievement and sit for . . . public school entrance exams?"

"One can be for exams," Mortimer said, "and against the class system, you know."

"I will not have everything I stand for in education, a lifetime's work, thrown up in my face at my own school. I will tolerate no counter-revolution at Beatrice Webb House."

Mortimer turned to Miss Ryerson. He touched her arm tenderly. "Does anybody else know about this?" he asked.

"Why, everybody in the school knows," Dr. Booker said. "Our nursery school teachers are up in arms. If, they say, Ryerson has been given such license, why can't they introduce toilet training in the nursery? *Potties.* At Beatrice Webb House. *Compulsory toilet training!* Might as well go the whole hog and bring in black shirts and jackboots for the whole staff."

"That's quite enough," Miss Ryerson said, rising. "Mortimer, would you be good enough to drive me home?"

"Certainly."

"But I'm not finished," Dr. Booker said.

"I'll wait for you outside the main entrance," Miss Ryerson said, and she left the office.

Dr. Booker brought out a bottle of Scotch and filled two glasses. "There are lads in the first form," he said, "who tremble with excitement when Miss Ryerson passes. They are killing themselves with self-imposed prep in the hope of being promoted to the second form a term earlier. Skipping grades. Can you imagine anything more distasteful to me?"

"What do you want me to do, exactly?"

"You've got to put it to her that if she's going to blow, it has to be all the boys in the second form or nothing. There will be no special treatment at Beatrice Webb House based on apparent intellectual superiority. You tell her it's all the boys or none."

"I couldn't do that."

"Would you like me to send for the boy who was dropped to fifth last Friday?"

"No."

"He's hooked."

"Poor, deprived kid."

"I could get matron to help out with him, but that good lady has enough to do."

"I'll bet."

"Well, then, will you speak to Miss Ryerson and tell her quite clearly what the options are?"

"If you insist, but I imagine she will have to be replaced."

"Thank you for coming, Mr. Griffin. And good afternoon."

"Good afternoon, Dr. Booker."

Miss Ryerson made tea for them in her bed-sitter.

"Sugar?"

"Two, please. Miss Ryerson, would you mind terribly if I smoked?"

"Must you?"

He nodded. "I want you to know," he said, "that I blame myself. I never should have allowed you to set foot in that iniquitous school."

"A teacher's duty is clear. She goes where she's needed most."

"There's nothing for it. You'll just have to resign now."

"Quit? Run away from a fight with the devil? Would that be . . . Christian?"

"God damn it, Miss Ryerson, you can't go around blowing school kids. It isn't done."

"Don't you dare," Miss Ryerson said evenly, "take the Lord's name in vain in my presence."

"Sorry."

"Are you dead set against blowing, Mortimer?"

"I wouldn't know how to answer that, Miss Ryerson. We've never discussed, well, sex –"

"*Put out that cigarette immediately.*"

"Yes."

"You ask me if you may smoke, I courteously acquiesce. Then you take the Lord's name in vain. And now you wish to discuss sex with me."

"I'm sorry."

"Now, you were saying?"

"Well, let me put it this way. I appreciate all that you must have been through at Beatrice Webb, but –"

"I tried everything. I emptied my whole bag of tricks. But I couldn't get them to keep quiet, let alone teach them. And then one day –" She broke off, her smile immensely self-satisfied, dreamy. "Well, you know."

"Blowing?"

"Yes. That did it. The old pooper has nothing to complain about. On the contrary. He should be pleased. It's like night and day, Mortimer. Won't you have a bickie?"

"No, thanks."

"A jam roll, then?"

"All right."

"Do you know what? I don't think he objects to what I'm doing for one little minute. It's their saying grace in the dining hall. Did you notice his smug atheist face, Mortimer? Fit to burst, it was."

"Yes, but all the same, Miss Ryerson –"

"Oh, I know it's unconventional. But it's such a small thing to do for the boys and they enjoy it so."

"It's dangerous, Miss Ryerson. I –"

"Now lookee here, son, I never swallow the stuff."

Mortimer coughed up his jam roll.

"In any event, I'm too old to have babies, aren't I?"

"Miss Ryerson, I never should have allowed –"

"You have nothing to reproach yourself for. Absolutely nothing. And, incidentally, Doug should make you proud."

"Well, thank you. He is learning more now and his manners have changed for the better, but, on the other hand –"

"You don't understand. What I mean to say is, well, he's quite the firmest lad in his form."

"Oh, my God. Jesus Christ!"

"*Mortimer!*"

"Miss Ryerson, let me put this to you. It's preposterous, I know, but Dr. Booker has asked me to tell you that if you're going to continue blowing, it has to be the whole form or nothing."

"He said that!"

"I told him you wished to resign."

"How dare you speak for me?"

"But, Miss Ryerson –"

"That's his proposition, is it?"

Mortimer nodded.

"Well then, you tell the old pooper, yes, I'll do it his way, but on one condition only. He lets me have the fifth form. The fourteen-year-olds. Another cup of tea, Mortimer?"

Twenty-Eight

FORTIFIED WITH BRANDY, Mortimer hopped a bus, alighting at the Albany.

"Well," Lord Woodcock said, "so you've come to see me at last."

Mortimer nodded feebly.

"Please sit down. I can see, well, that you have been ill."

Can you, Mortimer thought, startled.

"It's good to see you. Very good to see you."

As a matter of fact, Lord Woodcock was appalled. Mortimer was clean-shaven, but the nicks on his cheeks betrayed a shaky hand. Purple welts swelled under his bloodshot eyes. His shirt collar curled at the ends. His suit was unpressed.

"What is it you wished to speak to me about?"

"I won't mince words. I've always wanted you to be Oriole's next editor-in-chief. It was my wish that once Dino Tomasso had gone, you would take over. The Star Maker, I'm happy to say, more than concurs. It only remains for you to apologize to, um" – Lord Woodcock consulted a paper on his desk – "Mr. Jacob Shalinsky for the vile things you said to him and resume your classes in 'Reading for Pleasure.'"

Mortimer made no reply.

"Is it true that you said to Mr. Shalinsky that there are other problems besides the Jewish problem?"

"It was a stupid thing to say."

"Is it also true that you said to him, Damn your perverse Jewish soul?"

Mortimer lit one cigarette off another. "Jacob Shalinsky is an obnoxious little man. His friends make me sick."

"I appreciate your feelings –"

"Well, then?"

"But to an outsider this whole affair could only reek of racial prejudice."

"If anyone is suffering from prejudice it's me. There is such a thing, you know, as the tyranny of the minority."

"There have been letters of complaint. And a petition from your lecture class. The Star Maker is dead-set against bad publicity."

Mortimer sucked in a deep breath. "The Star Maker is a murderer, Lord Woodcock. He and Tomasso."

"I beg your pardon, sir?"

Mortimer told him about the Our Living History series. About Herr Dr. Manheim and the Frankfort efficiency team.

"How can you be anti-Semitic, on one hand, and prejudiced against Germans, on the other? I'm trying to understand you, but –"

"You are not taking me seriously."

"Are you a misanthrope, then?"

"They're murderers. Don't you understand?"

"The Our Living History is quite the most successful line we've had in years. Nobody has reproached you for not thinking of it first. It is most unbecoming, then, for you –"

"You think this is all sour grapes on my part."

"The competitive spirit, perhaps."

Mortimer repeated his story once more. He told Lord Woodcock what he had read in the file.

"How very interesting," Lord Woodcock said, surreptitiously removing the letter opener from his desk.

"You don't believe me, you old fool."

"Now, now, we mustn't excite ourselves, must we?"

"You think I'm crazy?"

"*Nobody is crazy.* I'm not a boor, you know. Some people are better-adjusted than others, that's all. Possibly, you've been drinking too much."

"Yes," Mortimer said, realizing there was no point, "that's the truth."

"Personal troubles?"

"A few."

"Pity."

Unaccountably, Mortimer began to laugh.

"Perhaps," Lord Woodcock said, "you should rest a little longer. Stay away from Oriole for a few more days. No need to rush things."

"Thank you."

"The Star Maker, you know, thinks the world of you –"

"I've got a marvy lymph system. And Polly Morgan is the same blood type."

"If you say so, I'm sure it's true. He thinks the world of you, Mortimer, and I'd hate to disabuse him."

"Good."

"Now about your lectures. Your Mr. Shalinsky was here to see me only yesterday –"

"After an ad for *Jewish Thought?*"

"Among other things. A most dedicated and erudite little man, I thought."

"He's a snake."

"Now, now. I thought it, um, interesting that he firmly believes that you are yourself, ah, of Hebraic origin."

"I'm a Presbyterian, Lord Woodcock. Like my father."

"I'm utterly opposed to prejudice. We must love one

another or die has always been my credo, but if there is one thing I abominate, Mortimer," he said, rising, "it is a Jewish anti-Semite."

Mortimer, to his amazement, gave Lord Woodcock a shove.

"Anger," Lord Woodcock said, his breath coming short, "sometimes betrays our deepest –"

Mortimer kicked the gold-tipped cane out from under him.

"You're sick –"

Which provoked a punch to Lord Woodcock's spilling belly.

"– mentally . . ."

Lord Woodcock gasped, sinking to the floor.

Next Mortimer took a taxi directly to The Eight Bells, where he consumed one brandy after another. Suddenly Polly Morgan stood before him. "Having a rough time?" she asked.

"Somewhat."

"If ever you want me," she said with a smile, "just whistle."

Twenty-Nine

IMMEDIATELY MORTIMER entered Polly Morgan's flat on Beaufort Street, already well fortified with Scotch, he was confronted by an outsize poster of Humphrey Bogart. "Play It Again, Sam." The dimly lit entry hall was lined with bookshelves, bookshelves sagging with volumes on the cinema, but when Polly took Mortimer's coat, disappearing briefly, and he stooped to pull out one of the books, he scraped his fingers. They were not books at all, but photographs of books pasted to the wall.

A framed black and white photograph of a Matisse hung over a mock fireplace, wherein plastic logs flickered red and orange, lit by a revolving light inside. Crackle, crackle, went the tape that was turned on automatically with the fire. There were other framed stills of paintings on the wall, all of them in black and white, but there was only one original. A first-edition color poster for *Gone with the Wind*, Gable scooping Vivien Leigh into his arms, Atlanta flaring red behind.

"V. Fleming," Polly said. "Selznick, M-G-M. 1939. 41,200,000. *Variety*'s all-time grosser until *Sound of Music*."

"What's that?"

"*Sound of Music.* R. Wise. 20th. 1965. 42,500,000. What about a drink?"

"I'd love one."

"You look sad," she said, handing him a martini.

"Do I?"

"Don't tell me. . . . Way back, a million light years ago maybe, you started out on a big white charger, waving a flag."

Mortimer watched, agog, as Polly brushed the hint of a tear from her suddenly watery blue eyes.

"Now your arms are tired," she continued, "the charger is in the glue factory and you're sitting on a bomb, a ticking bomb . . ."

Mortimer emptied his glass. "Would it be possible to have another?"

"Let me."

The candle-lit table was set for two. One red rose stood in a narrow vase and there was a bottle of champagne in a silver bucket. Polly put on a record, some Chopin from *A Song to Remember*. She looked fetching, maddeningly desirable, in her white mini-sheath, but Mortimer, even though he fed his imagination on pictures of lechery, felt no upspringing whatsoever. "You look absolutely gorgeous," he said, tottering toward her.

"Don't touch me," she pleaded. "I shan't be able to think, if you touch me."

All the same, he kissed her, indelicately driving her body against him, trying to arouse himself.

"Oooo," she moaned.

"I'm sorry. I shouldn't have done that."

"Sorry? No, no. I guess I've been wanting you to do just that for a long time."

"Really?" he said, pleased, then, remembering his condition, was alarmed.

"I wish . . . oh, I wish," she whispered.

"What?"

"I wish we had met ten years ago."

A month ago would have done nicely, he thought bitterly.

"No," she corrected herself. "Ten years ago, well, we were

two different people, we wouldn't have –" She stopped short. "Wrong again. I'd have loved you in any time, any place."

"*Loved* me," he exclaimed.

All the tenderness went out of Polly's face. She seemed immensely irritated with herself. "Did I do that badly?" she asked. "Was I standing in the wrong place?"

"What's that?"

"It's just that this side of my face – *yikes!* My dinner!" she said, possibly to cover her embarrassment.

Mortimer followed her into the tiny planned kitchen. Testing his reactions, he kissed her hopefully on the nape of the neck.

"Oh, no, you don't," she squealed pleasurably. "You just control yourself until after dinner."

Until after dinner.

Taking him by the hand, Polly led him back into the living room, kissed him, and pushed him back on the sofa. "I won't be long," she said.

Mortimer's hands began to tremble. *Until after dinner.* Oh God, he thought, to be offered Polly on a plate and – and – there's no justice. Mortimer caught a glimpse of her through the kitchen porthole, poring over her *Larousse*, tapping her teeth with her finger. But who would have known, he thought, arguing with himself. After all, everybody's had a go at her and nobody . . . I'm reading things into the situation. Why, she's a virgin. There's nothing to worry about, absolutely nothing. But, rising to pour himself another martini, he happened to peek into the bedroom and what he saw made his heart leap. On the bedside table there stood a bottle of wine and two glasses. Mortimer sank back on the sofa, closed his eyes, and prayed.

He had, it seemed to him, only rested for a minute, two at the most, when the next thing he knew . . . they were lying on pillows in front of the fire, she in his arms, a tray with coffee and brandy on the floor beside them.

"I'm sorry about the sauce," she said. "It just didn't work."

"No, no, it was delicious."

Craning his neck, Mortimer stared at the table. The candle had burned down to a flickering stump. The bottle of champagne floated overturned in the silver bucket. There was hardly any roast left on the meat board. And yet – and yet – Mortimer could have sworn he hadn't eaten. Drunkenness made him forgetful, but not *that* forgetful. Besides, he was still hungry. He was bloody famished, in fact.

"What are we going to do," Polly asked, running a long cool finger over his lips, "about us?"

"What do you mean?"

"I wouldn't want to hurt . . . Joyce."

He and Joyce, he explained, somewhat irritated, were no longer living together.

"You needn't explain," she said, running a hand down his side.

"Um, one minute. Perhaps there's something I should explain. About me."

"But there's no need. I know, I know."

He had thought only Doug knew, and Ziggy, but obviously –

"You've been living in the same house, you and Joyce, strangers under the same roof. You've been sharing a bed, but there's no love in your lovemaking. . . . Once you could talk to each other, but not any more. . . . *Listen!*"

Outside, somewhere in the night, a bird called to its mate. Then she was in his arms again, passionately this time, and Mortimer, his anguish total, began falteringly, "Wait, there's something I *must* tell you . . . I'm sort of not well recently . . . *unfit*. I –" He feigned dizziness. "If I could only shut my eyes and rest, just for a minute, please."

But when he opened his eyes she was gone.

"Polly?"

He found her luxuriating on the bed, nude, sleepy-eyed,

satiated. She scooped up the sheet, covering herself, holding it coyly to her bosom. "It was super," she said. "Absolutely super. Was it super for you too, darling?"

"Well, yes."

"Was it never like this for you before?"

"*No!*"

"You're such a bad liar. I love you for that."

"But I'm telling the truth, God damn it."

"Yes, you are. That's exactly what I mean. If you were lying, I could tell from your face."

He sat down on the bed beside her and reached for the bottle of wine. To his amazement, it was empty. The ashtray on the bedside table was full. He scrutinized the butts. Yes, they were his brand.

"Was life ever this good?"

But I've still got my clothes on, he thought, his head aching. "No," he said.

"Am I your whole life to you, Mortimer?"

He didn't answer.

"No, my sweet," she answered for him, "and I wouldn't want to be."

"Why the hell not?" he asked, irritation, bewilderment, ripening into anger.

"If I were your whole life," she said, "that would mean you would die without me."

"Would I?"

"I couldn't bear that responsibility."

"Oh, my head, my poor head."

"Let's live for love, Mortimer, you and I," she said, hugging him. "Let's not die for it." Then she fell away from him and was asleep almost immediately.

Mortimer tottered into the living room and stared once more at the table where they appeared to have eaten together. The champagne bottle, he saw, was truly empty but, in the kitchen, he was unable to find any used pots or pans or soiled dishes. In fact all he found in the kitchen was stacks and stacks of film scripts, shooting scripts complete with camera directions. Mortimer found his coat and let himself out of Polly's flat. Outside, he noticed two black-suited men seated in a parked Rover. He stopped a taxi and clambered inside wearily. The Rover started up and followed, but at a distance.

Migod.

Thirty

"HELLO, HELLO. MAY I speak with the Star Maker, please."

"Who is it calling?"

"Mortimer Griffin."

"One moment, please," Miss Mott said.

There was a pause.

"Well, hello there."

"Star Maker?"

"At your service."

"I've thought it over. I'll take the job."

"Are you sure, Mortimer?"

"Absolutely. It's definite."

"Good boy."

"Oh, incidentally, Star Maker, I've kept your secrets. All your secrets, I haven't spoken to anyone. Just like I promised."

"Your word is your bond."

"Yes, sir."

"Is that all, then?"

"Oh, well, I suppose I should tell you I had something of a tiff with Lord Woodcock."

"What happened?"

"What happened?"

"Yes."

"He hasn't mentioned it, then?"

"No."

"It's very funny."

"How come?"

"Well, I was drunk, see, my mind's a complete blank, but I think I hit him."

"Not to worry."

"The embarrassing thing is I can't remember a thing I said to him. But he's not to be trusted."

"Is that so?"

"Lord Woodcock has his virtues, God knows, but he's a compulsive liar. I can't tell you how anxious I am to get started at Oriole."

"Good boy. When can we meet and talk again?"

"Any day now, Star Maker. I'll call you the day after tomorrow."

"Splendid."

"Meanwhile, don't you worry about me. My lips are sealed."

"You have my complete trust, Mortimer."

"You too, Star Maker. Goodbye now."

"Toodle-loo."

Mortimer stepped out of the telephone booth and walked slowly toward The Eight Bells, the Rover following after. Once inside, he scooted downstairs to the Gents, and out the back door.

The first travel agency he came to was on Oxford Street.

"One way," the clerk said. "Economy or first class?"

"Economy."

"Two tickets to Toronto would come to two hundred and five pounds."

"Thank you."

We'll need a stake, Mortimer thought, continuing down Oxford Street. A nice hunk of cash. In a hurry.

Thirty-One

"TONIGHT, FANS," DIG began gleefully, "we have a rare and distinct pleasure in store. We have with us in the studio a holder of . . . the *Victoria Cross*."

This brought forth jeers and hoots. "Here's a hot one coming up," somebody said.

"The Victoria Cross, fans, is awarded *for valor*. 'For conspicuous bravery or devotion to duty in the presence of the enemy.'"

Superimposed on the screen was the face of Peter Sellers, his eyes crossed under a battle helmet as he peered down the wrong end of a rifle. Laughter exploded in the studio.

"Its inscription reads '*For the Brave.*'"

On screen, David Warner as *Morgan* ran backwards, the action speeded up.

"During World War II," Dig continued, "in the six years of violence that was to make" – here he cupped a hand over his mouth, swallowing a giggle – "a brave new world for us cats . . ."

The atomic bomb exploded on screen.

". . . just fourteen Canadians in all won the Victoria Cross, and five of them paid for it with their lives."

The opening bars of "God Save the Queen" was played off key by the Berliner Ensemble Band.

"One of the survivors . . . Captain, once Major, Mortimer Griffin, is with us here tonight."

Tssst-tssst-tssst.

"But, first of all, let me fill you in on some of the other Victoria Cross winners. One of them, formerly a captain, has said, quote, I enjoyed the war."

Dig's voice ran over a superimposed panning shot of a military graveyard, an endless vista of crosses.

"It was like a game of cowboys and Indians. The only difference is we were using live ammunition, unquote."

In the ensuing laughter Mortimer noted that Dig had neglected to add that the captain in question had lost both his legs in the action for which he was decorated.

"Another," Dig said, "writes me that his favorite reading is . . . *James Bond!*"

Finally, Dig got to Mortimer. An old photograph of Mortimer in his army uniform was flashed on the screen. A decidedly comic, hollow military drumbeat in the background.

"On August 8, 1944, Major Mortimer Griffin of the 2nd Canadian Infantry was in command of a battalion in the Falaise pocket. Heavily outnumbered, his armored support battered, he was attacking an enemy position of vital importance. If he took it he would cut off the retreat of not one, but two" – Dig raised two fingers – "*Nazi-rat* regiments. . . ."

Action frames from American wartime comic books were superimposed on screen.

"POW! KAZAAM! BOOM!"

Laughter rocked the studio.

"His superiors ordered Griffin to pull back, but the clean-cut young major replied, according to press reports, 'Retreat, heck.' "

Dig swung his chair round to smile encouragingly at Mortimer. "Was it actually 'retreat, heck,' you said . . . or was it something less, um, *wholesome?*"

"Something less wholesome."

"Major Griffin, according to the press report I have here, told his men, 'There are enemy in front of us, enemy behind us, and enemy on our flanks. There's only one place to go, fellas. Onward.' In the ensuing action, the Canadians lost 132 men, but the . . . *Nazi-rat* retreat was cut off and as a result 2,000 prisoners were taken. Major Griffin, in a conspicuous act of . . . um . . . *bravery* . . . crawled to a knoll exposed to enemy machine-gun fire – *Rat-tat-tat . . . rat-tat-tat* – and rescued a wounded corporal. His corporal. Wounded twice in the legs, he refused to be evacuated until his men had been seen to and reinforcements had arrived."

Laughter began to rise in the studio. "Wait," Dig said, choking it off with a wave of his arm, "it gets better. . . . Major Griffin's commanding officer, one of the first on the scene, said – we are assured in Canadian Press dispatches – with a grin from ear to ear, 'For disobeying orders, Griffin, I'm stripping you to the rank of captain, effective immediately. But for amazing Canuck bravery in the face of a superior enemy force I'm recommending you for – for' – Drums, please," Dig asked.

The camera dollied in on the drummer, an old man with a Beatle haircut wearing a uniform obviously bought at "I Was Lord Kitchener's Valet."

". . . '*for the Victoria Cross.*' "

Laughter was unconfined.

"Before we question Major Griffin about details, who, you may well ask, is this brave soldier?"

Dig glowered at the studio audience: the laughter subsided.

"Born in Caribou, Ontario, Major Griffin became a Queen's Scout at the age of fourteen."

This brought forth yet another explosion of laughter, which Mortimer didn't comprehend because he couldn't see the monitor on which there was now projected a blowup of another Queen's Scout, Charles Joseph Whitman, who on

August 7, 1966, climbed the University of Texas Tower, rifle in hand, and shot everyone in sight, killing thirteen people and wounding thirty-one.

"In high school, Mortimer Griffin won a Rotary Public Speaking Award and was voted –"

Now Richard Nixon's face filled the screen.

"– Most Likely to Succeed."

On and on went the potted, incriminating biography. Finally Dig turned to Mortimer again, his grin infectious.

"Well now, Major, what would you say if I could demonstrate to you, statistically proven, that the average I.Q. of Victoria Cross winners is more than slightly below the national average –"

"But –"

"– and considerably lower than that of deserters. What, if anything, would you say to that?"

"We didn't get the medal for I.Q."

"Quite. But it does say something, doesn't it, about the nature of *physical* courage and its relationship to imagination, the failure thereof."

Women applauded until their hands ached. Men stamped their feet.

"Tell me, Griffin, during the war did you kill any Germans?"

"Yes."

"And how do you feel about that . . . now?"

"Well, that was the war. We were at war then."

"Quite. And you were only obeying orders?"

"Yes . . ."

"*Like Adolf Eichmann?*"

"Hold on there!"

"Just another little cog in the wheel, weren't you?"

Tssst-tssst-tssst.

"Now, your citation reads that you crawled out on to a

knoll, under enemy fire, to rescue one of your men. A corporal. Your very own corporal. Right?"

"Yes."

"Not bent, are you, Griffin?"

"I beg your pardon?"

"Did you have carnal knowledge of the corporal?"

"No!"

"Then why did you crawl out to save him, for Christ's sake!"

"It just seemed the thing to do."

"Come on, come on. You're more articulate than that."

"I was there. I saw him. I couldn't pretend I hadn't seen him. I had to go after him."

"So you saved his life?"

"It wasn't my fault."

"Griffin, what if I told you that the man whose life you saved has since slit his wife's throat and raped his eight-year-old girl?"

"It wouldn't be true."

"It wouldn't be *factually* true. But, if it were the case, wouldn't your action – like all our actions, good or bad – be absurd? Don't you, an intelligent man, recognize our lives as absurd?"

"No. I believe in the possibilities within each of us for goodness."

"For *what?*"

"Goodness . . ."

"*Louder, please.*"

"*Goodness!*"

"Griffin, to return to your rescue of the man on the knoll. You said, quote, I saw him. I couldn't pretend I hadn't seen him. *I had to go after him*, unquote. Right?"

"Yes."

"You a conformist?"

"What?"

"Don't suffer from a death wish, do you?"

"No."

"And so, in other words, it would have required more courage, moral courage, to hold back. I mean to say, if you hadn't been so worried about . . . looking bad . . . about riding with the herd . . . if you had been absolutely honest with yourself, you would have held back. Yes or no?"

Mortimer hesitated.

"*He is* –" a man in the audience hollered.

"*– shittier than the rest of us*," another fan returned.

"Wait," Dig cautioned. "Give him a chance to answer my question."

"The answer is I did the necessary thing."

A man rose, cupping his hands to his mouth. "*Bullsh* –"

"Fans, wait! Hold it! The fact is Mortimer Griffin is no phony."

Studio fans, unsettled, began to mutter among themselves.

"He isn't shittier than we are."

The camera played on the studio audience just as an irate young couple got up and walked out.

"What's going on here?"

"Dig's a sellout."

"You can't believe in anything these days."

Another couple left. And another. Satisfied now, Dig, clutching his microphone, came round his desk to confront his rebellious followers. "Mortimer Griffin," he began, breaking off as he was seized by a paroxysm of laughter. "The major here –" Dig clutched his stomach, helpless. "The captain –" Tears rolled down his cheeks. "Mortimer Griffin is a – a – a – a *hero!*"

In the control room, the director and his crew sat bolt upright. "Hero" had not been said on British television for years. Would they be cut off?

"He's a fucking . . . *hero*," Dig said, wiping his face.

Pandemonium.

"You can never count old Dig out."

"Good old Dig."

"Imagine," a man said, slapping his cheek. "A hero."

"Poor dumb bastard."

As Mortimer, followed by the camera, slunk offstage, nobody laughed. Nobody scoffed. He was not ridiculed. Swingers, after all, were not without pity.

Thirty-Two

"WELL, LOOK WHO'S here. Mr. Chickenshit himself. Diana," he hollered, beginning to flex his hands, "bring out the gloves."

"No gloves, damn it. I've got to talk to you, Hy. It's about Oriole – the Star Maker – I'm in serious danger."

"That's not what I hear. I hear you're the new editor-in-chief. That means I'm looking for a new job, Dr. Himmler."

"Please hear me out, Hy, you're just about my last hope."

Briefly, Hy's belligerent manner faltered. He considered Mortimer with something like his former regard. "Shoot," he said.

Mortimer, relieved, was just about to begin his story when a bald, pear-shaped man, sucking an enormous cigar, stepped out of the living room. He walked toward Mortimer, his soft ringed hand outstretched.

"My father," Hy said in a failing voice. "Paw, Mortimer Griffin. A friend of mine. Once."

"Put it there, Morty. You've known my Hymie for years, haven't you? Well, maybe you can tell me what's wrong with him?"

"But Hy's a splendid chap. Just the sort you can count on in a moment of need."

"And always walking around with that expression like somebody was going to take a scissors like this," Mr. Rosen said, demonstrating with two extended fingers, "and snip his bleeding cock off."

"Hy's been my best friend for years and years."

"Listen, I'm not saying my Hymie's a shmuck. I only wish I had his head for the market."

"*Hy?*"

"When he was younger and playing only for fun he picked winners nine out of ten. Hymie knows his onions. He's got a good Jewish head on his shoulders."

"The capacity to judge the market has nothing to do with one's racial origins."

"You got kiddies of your own, Morty, or are you a nit with a social conscience like Hymie here?"

"I've told my father a hundred times that world conditions being what they are, it would be madness to bring a child into –"

"World conditions, my arse. You want to make Diana happy or you want she should end up like Cousin Sadie with twitches and headaches for no reason and the insides, God forbid, being scraped out twice a –"

"Somebody ought to tell you the facts about strontium 90."

"Think of the pleasure it would give me to have a grandchild. A Bar Mitzvah boy."

"Even if we had a child there'd be no Bar Mitzvah. I've told you a hundred times, Paw, Diana and I are atheists."

"Facts of life. Your Diana can be an atheist. Your friend Morty can be an atheist. You can only be a bloody Jewish atheist."

"We will not burden any child of ours with outmoded tribal customs. That's final, Paw."

"Education, that's what's giving him such a pain in the *kishkes*. Here's a goy, we'll ask him. Isn't it true that your kind has more respect for a Jew who is a Jew? Take Rothschild, for instance. He would never buy or sell on the Sabbath. Or take me. On Yom Kippur I fast. I go to *shul*."

"You drive there and that's against the law."

"I'm not a fanatic, you know."

"You go to the synagogue to discuss business. Not to worship."

"There's something wrong with talking business?" Mr. Rosen asked Mortimer.

"He doesn't know. He's condescending to you, Paw."

"Listen," Mr. Rosen said, seizing Mortimer by the lapels, "I like you. You're highly intelligent, I can see. Wednesday I'm taking Hy and Diana to dinner. You're his friend and he never gives me a chance to meet any. You come too. There'll be plenty to drink. The best."

"My father never invites a Gentile out without first assuring him there will be plenty to drink. A ghetto compulsion."

"You don't drink?"

"Of course I do."

"See?"

"And I'd be glad to come."

"You don't have to prove anything to me, you bastard."

"But, Hy, I –"

"And I won't have you patronizing my father. He thinks you're colorful, Paw. A character."

"No kidding," Mr. Rosen said, beaming.

"*You're* ashamed of him."

Hy started to say something, stopped, and grabbed his coat. "I'm going out for a breath of air," he said.

"Hy, wait! I need you."

He slammed the door.

"*Hy!*"

"He's a sensitive boy," Mr. Rosen said. "Don't you think?"

Thirty-Three

POLLY COULDN'T UNDERSTAND what document he was working on so secretively. Typing it over and over again. Or why he drank so much and double-locked the doors. Neither could she understand why he pretended to be ill, avoiding Oriole House. Everybody knew he was going to take over from Tomasso. You'd think he'd be proud.

"Men," she said, ruffling his hair.

"What?"

"Don't hate me," she whispered.

"But I adore you," he said.

"I'm pregnant."

"That's bloody impossible! One, I've only been staying here for a few nights and two, let's face it, Polly, we've never actually –"

"No, you won't hate me. If I know you, you beautiful idiot, tomorrow you'll be handing out cigars everywhere. You'll be off to Harrod's to buy him the biggest panda going . . . and you'll be putting him down for Eton." Polly chuckled lovingly. "By the time you get done with it, I will have had nothing to do with it at all."

"But, God damn it, Polly –"

"Oh, how I love you when you're angry."

As soon as she had gone to sleep, Mortimer poured himself

a drink and went off to the kitchen in search of ice cubes. Once more, he was struck by the screenplays stacked here, there, and everywhere. No: it couldn't be. And yet . . . Mortimer reached for the first screenplay. He sat by the kitchen table all night, consuming one screenplay after another, understanding coming to him at last.

The following evening Mortimer led Polly across the river to a decrepit, sleazy street. Unmistakably a back street.

"I feel like a murderer," she said, sobbing.

"It can't be helped, darling."

"Don't come any farther with me."

"As you wish." He handed her a thick envelope. "You go to No. 83 and ask for Dr. O'Hara. You hand him this."

Mortimer watched her, his eyes tracking, as she continued alone down the endless street, slowly, slowly, running her gloved hand along a wrought-iron fence, just as she had done as a child. . . .

Concentrating on holding the glove in a tight shot, as it were, Mortimer detected the contaminating grit of experience rubbing off on its pure, bored, overrich whiteness. Finally, he concentrated on Polly starting up the steps to No. 83.

Ordering another in the pub, thinking it over, Mortimer regretted that it wasn't autumn. Possibly, she had missed the falling leaves. Oh, well, can't have everything, and he took his time returning to the flat on Beaufort Street, allowing her time to change and adjust mentally for the next scene, the obligatory dissolve to the bedroom.

As he had anticipated, she said, "I feel dirty."

As was expected of him, he replied, "Yes, I know," but emptily.

Oh, how he adored Polly, creature of a generation, but living with her was, nevertheless, a mixed pleasure. If, for instance, she looked up a complicated meal in *Larousse*, he had to reconcile himself to a hasty sandwich secretly consumed in the toilet, for she was bound to cut from pondering the sauce to serving coffee and brandy, just as she dissolved from his cupping a breast to the gratifying pillow talk that followed the most satisfying lovemaking.

One sun-filled but rather wintry afternoon, she insisted that he take her to Richmond Park, where they ate a picnic lunch.

"You look absolutely ravishing," he said.

"When we are old," she said, "I want you to always remember me like this, the sun catching fire in my hair . . ."

"The look in your eyes," he continued for her, "ten fathoms deep."

Reaching for her hand, he pulled her to him. Then, for he was in a considerate mood, just as he reached for the top button of her dress, he spun her around, so that she could cut away, so to speak, over his shoulder . . . to the stags locking horns in the distance.

Living in sin, Polly called it, but the affair, such as it was, had only been consummated on the wide screen of her imagination, which, alas, suited him – suited him too damn well, considering his condition.

Mortimer's happiness was blunted by an overriding anxiety. As things stood, Polly accepted him as the consummate lover. But week by week the movies were leaving less to the imagination, the love scenes were becoming more explicit, and so surely it was only a question of time before Ziggy's artistic dream came true and it would be possible to show fucking on the screen. Then, what? Then she would come to realize he wasn't up to the big scene, and she would look elsewhere for a man, a real man, to track in on her.

"I'm your mistress," she said, dancing across the room, "and I don't care if the whole world knows."

"You can shout it from the rooftops," he replied, looking up from his typing.

If Polly didn't do precisely that, she did at least let everybody know that she was living with Mortimer, the most demanding and masterful of lovers, and naturally this especially delighted him. Oh, to be the envy of Oriole, of all publishing in fact, for there wasn't an editor under sixty who hadn't had a go at Polly Morgan, but only Griffin had won her favors. Such as they were, he added to himself in dark or drunken moments.

"Typedy-type-type," Polly said. "What ever are you working at?"

"An indictment, if you must know," Mortimer said, rising, as he folded papers into two separate long brown envelopes.

Polly watched him get into his coat. "Don't tell me you're actually going into Oriole this morning."

"No. I've got business elsewhere. See you later, darling."

Across the street, the Rover waited, the two black-suited men inside. I should get these papers to Joyce first. Or Hy, he thought. But, on impulse, Mortimer walked right up to the Rover. "Okay," he said, "let's get it over with. Take me to *it*."

Thirty-Four

"HELLO THERE. GREETINGS."

The Star Maker sat up in bed, knitting, a patch over the right eye. The bassinet Mortimer had last seen at the studio stood under the window in the Star Maker's suite at the Clinic.

"Star Maker," Mortimer demanded, "why are you still having me followed?"

"Sit down, my boy. Pour yourself a drink."

Mortimer eagerly sloshed brandy into a glass. "Why are you here?" he asked.

The Star Maker blushed, actually blushed.

"I will be operating out of here for at least nine months to come."

"*Nine?*"

The Star Maker chortled, swollen breasts shaking. "But it can't show yet," the Star Maker said, flushed with pleasure.

"What can't show yet?"

"That I'm pregers."

"*Pregnant? You?*"

"Well, let's not put the cart before the horse. However, I can reveal this much. I'm very, very overdue this month."

"*Overdue!*"

"Mn. Join me in a cigar?"

Mortimer, his hands shaking, lit a cigar for himself and one for the Star Maker. The Star Maker inhaled deeply and set the knitting aside.

"Star Maker, may I ask you a personal question?"

"Shoot, dear."

"Are you a man or a woman?"

"But don't you know? Haven't you guessed? I," the Star Maker said, "am a modern medical miracle."

Mortimer hastily poured himself another brandy.

"There are many sexes," the Star Maker said, "and gradients on the Kinsey scale, categories within categories. Hetero, homo, Lesbian, the mundane variants, are all familiar to you, I'm sure. But there are the more complicated genders. There are the transvestites and, above all, the transsexuals. Tiresias changed himself into a woman because he felt that the woman's kicks during intercourse were ten to the man's one, and, damn it, he had the odds very nearly right. The East Indian King, Mahabharata, transformed himself for the same hedonistic reasons. Nero . . . well he's still a dodgy case, but history bounds with more recent examples. The Chevalier d'Éon, for instance, lived forty-nine years as a man and thirty-four as a woman. L'Abbé d'Entragues had a shot at feminine facial beauty by submitting to frequent facial bleedings. A certain Mlle. Jenny Savalette de Lange died at Versailles in 1858 and was found out to be a man. More recently there was the sensational case of Christine Jorgensen, born a man, transformed into a woman by a with-it Scandinavian doctor. The true transsexual, Mortimer, is a man born into a woman's body or vice versa. The most unhappy of God's creatures until he or she is operated on.

"I first became fascinated by these unfortunates some fifty years ago, when transsexual surgery was still in the Kitty Hawk stage. And then, maybe ten years ago, I learned of the genius of Casablanca, Dr. Georges Burou, who has been of such help to TS's of both sexes . . . though, characteristically, I'm afraid, the Russians are miles ahead of us in penis making –"

"In *what* making?"

"I knew that would interest you."

"*Why should it interest me, you bastard?*"

"Because obviously, my dear, if they can build from scratch, sometimes requiring as many as thirty operations, then they can also add to what is already there, don't you think?"

Mortimer stared into his glass.

"Whatever you decide, you must say no to the prosthesis."

"To the what?"

"Artificial penises. They go in for it a lot in the States. It's *plastic*, Mortimer. Déclassé. No damn fun at all, and then you've got to worry during the summer heat waves, electric blankets in winter are out of course, and so are hot baths and –"

"I have absolutely no interest in the matter."

The Star Maker was seemingly unconvinced. "To return to the great Burou. He, needless to say, doesn't mess about with plastic pricks at all. He has been of enormous help to the male TS, who wishes to be womanized. He has in fact again and again made the most marvy cunts, working with nothing more than a drippy, wizened old prick. He inverts the skin, don't you see? There's nothing quite like it for a new vaginal canal, because the penis, any old penis, is so rich in nerve ends and –"

"I don't want to talk about it any more, please."

"Well, I had been keeping a file on TS surgery for years and at the same time I began to worry about my own mortality. You do worry, you know, when the younger fellas begin to go. Churchill, Maugham, Beaverbrook . . . I knew morbid days, Mortimer. Even with my mobile hospital and spare-parts men at my beck and call, could I die too?"

"*Too?*"

"Exactly how I felt. Oh, Lord, what a waste, I thought. And me with no heir."

"Couldn't you marry?"

"For money? I have more than I can count."

"For love, then?"

"But, my dear child, I only love me."

The Star Maker leaned forward and Mortimer relit the cigar.

"Great ideas, my boy, are born accidentally. Newton and the apple, Watt and the teakettle. . . . Well, one day Dino Tomasso and I had a tiff, over his coming to London, and he actually said to me, Go fuck yourself, Star Maker. . . . *Go fuck yourself, go fuck yourself*. . . . What a brilliant notion. Why not, I thought. Do you follow me so far?"

Mortimer nodded.

"If they can make cunts for men and outfit girls with cocks, well, why not everything, the whole shebang, within one human body?"

"What about . . . defecation?" was all Mortimer could think of asking.

"Through a pouch. Here."

"Christ."

"It's taken countless operations . . . set-backs . . . grafts that wouldn't take . . . more and more spare-parts men . . . secrecy . . . Until, well, here I am, ducks," the Star Maker said, raising arms, one reaching higher than the other.

Mortimer felt his stomach rising within him.

"Since God, the first self-contained creator, Mortimer, I am now able to reproduce myself. I will have a son."

"What if it's a girl?"

"But I fully intend to have more than one. Only children are so spoiled, don't you think?"

"I don't believe a word of it. You're insane."

"Fifty years ago would you have believed in men flying into space?"

Mortimer didn't answer.

"There is inner space as well as outer, you see. And it's fun, oh it's such fun. In all my years, I have enjoyed nothing more than making love to me," the Star Maker said, embracing, nuzzling upper arms, kissing, licking.

Mortimer averted his eyes.

"It's so good to be able to give it to myself regular. What's wrong?"

"I'm going to be ill."

"Over there, honey," the Star Maker said, indicating a door.

Mortimer rushed, retching, for the toilet, where he was sick again and again. On the glass shelf over the sink, after-shave lotion and a bottle of Joy stood side by side. Mortimer finally lit a cigarette, washed, and returned to find the Star Maker sipping a glass of warm milk.

"And how are you?" the Star Maker said. "Have you been able to get it up since our last chat?"

Mortimer glared.

"Forgive me. Of course you have. Polly Morgan is positively blooming."

"Star Maker, I have only one reason for being here. To tell you that I'm resigning."

"Well, you have changed your tune, haven't you? On the phone you said you were eager to take over. It's definite, you said."

"I don't want to work for you."

"A better offer?"

"Hardly."

"I see."

"I will not repeat your secrets to anyone."

"You're a man of your word."

"However, I have taken the precaution of setting down what I know about the Our Living History series. I have left this information somewhere in a sealed envelope. If any harm comes to me or Polly Morgan –"

"What nonsense!"

"Your men follow me wherever I go."

"Why, that's frightful. I had no idea, I'll put a stop to that immediately."

"You'd better. Because if you don't –"

"Please don't threaten me, Mortimer. Let's remain friends."

Mortimer lit one cigarette off another.

"I still wish you'd take over Oriole from Tomasso. You look poorly, son. Why not think it over a bit longer?"

"My decision is final."

"Well, in that case there is nothing more for me to do than wish you the best of luck."

"And call off your men, please."

"I will do nothing to harm you, my boy, so long as you give me your word not to speak of my private affairs."

"Gladly."

"No hard feelings, eh, Mortimer?"

"None."

"You'll come to the christening, then."

"I couldn't bear to miss it. So long, Star Maker."

The Star Maker blew him a kiss and then pressed the buzzer for Miss Mott.

"Yes?"

"Get me Tomasso on the phone. Instantly."

The Star Maker explained to Tomasso exactly what had to be done.

"Yes," Tomasso said. "Can do. Right away." He hung up and dialed long distance. "Get me Frankfort," he said.

Thirty-Five

WHOM COULD HE ENTRUST the envelope to? Joyce, after all, was still his wife. They had taken vows together.

"Well," she said expansively, "I hear that you and Polly Morgan –"

"It's none of your business."

"Perhaps not. But I'm so glad to know that you can obviously get it up again."

"Again and again. We tend to overdo it, rather."

"Don't you think she's a bit young for you?"

Mortimer jumped up to look out of the window. No Rover. No black-suited men. Relieved, he whacked the window open. "I hope you don't mind," he said, staring at the matted tangle under her armpits and wondering if it would ever stop growing. "Incidentally," he continued merrily, "if you should want a divorce –"

"Divorce? What ever for?"

"Well, I'd hate to stand between you and old Ziggy, you know."

"Ziggy," she said snidely, "would never marry me."

"Ah ha."

"He respects me too much. He wouldn't contaminate our relationship by having me become a possession, a chattel. He wants me to remain free to love him."

"How very, very nice for you. May I see Dougie now?"

"He's already asleep."

"Well, then," he said, rising.

"Wait. My congratulations, darling."

"What ever for?"

"Your life's dream come true. I understand you're going to take over Oriole."

"You understand wrong. As usual. I've resigned."

"You've what?"

"That ought to please Hy Rosen, don't you think?"

"What a dreadful thing to say. Hy's your best friend."

"My best friend? Wake up. He doesn't even talk to me any more."

"If he feels hurt I'm afraid he's got good reason."

"You mean I'm an anti-Semite?"

"Mortimer, how could you have written that article on Chagall for *Jewish Thought?*"

"What's wrong with it?"

"Did you have to call it 'A Jewish Answer to Picasso'? Hy's indignant. He thinks that was so cheap of you. He –"

"I'll kill that Shalinsky. I'll murder him."

"Mortimer, wait."

But it was no use. He was off. He was lucky enough to trap a taxi immediately. Another car pulled out after him, right after him, but it wasn't a Rover. There were no black-suited men inside. I'm jumpy, that's all.

Thirty-Six

"How sweet of you to visit me, Griffin. After our little differences. So, how are you?"

"Oh, fine. Just fine. And you?"

"Like this, like that."

Shalinsky sat at his kitchen table correcting proofs. His trouser legs were rolled up and his feet were soaking in a basin of steaming water. A heap of old clothes was stacked on the chair beside him.

"Do you also deal in old clothes?" Mortimer asked, his purpose to insult.

"I collect them. I send parcels to my writers. In the Iron Curtain countries, you know, it's no picnic for our Yiddish poets."

"But how on earth can you afford it?" Mortimer asked, indicating the pile of tinned foods on the table.

"It's a struggle, Griffin. A real struggle. But the artist's lot, need I tell you, has always been the same. Anyway Levitt – he prints *Jewish Thought* for me – also gives me work as a salesman. I go from office to office. You know, letterheads, greeting cards, dance programs. . . . My feet aren't what they used to be. I do a lot by phone now, but. . . . Well, the commission isn't half bad." He smiled stoically. "Would you like to see my *bureau?*"

Mortimer followed Shalinsky into a small, stifling room.

Over the rolltop desk was a framed portrait of Chaim Nachman Bialik. Yellowing newspapers, magazines, and proofs were heaped high on two chairs. Books were stacked everywhere. Shalinsky opened his filing cabinet and Mortimer had to jump back to avoid puffs of dust. Shalinsky pulled out a letter and handed it to Mortimer.

My Dear Shalinsky,

Thank you for sending me your magazine. I enjoyed reading it.

Sincerely yours,
Albert Einstein

There were more, equally terse but polite notes from others, including Theodor Herzl, John Garfield, FDR, Harold Laski, Al Jolson, and King George VI.

"In that issue there was a comparative study I'm sure he enjoyed of the House of Windsor and the House of David. *Of Cabbages and Kings* by I. M. Sinclair. At the time it was very widely quoted."

Shalinsky showed Mortimer some of his own published work, letters to the editor that had appeared in the *New Statesman*, the *Guardian* and the *Observer*. Protests against the release of the film version of *Oliver Twist*, pleas for impoverished Yiddish writers, a demand for a ban on East European goods until imprisoned poets were released. "I have published more letters to the editor than any other writer in England," he said.

"I'm impressed, really I am."

"Ach, we're both in the same boat."

"How do you mean?"

"I'm a writer *manqué*. Like you."

Restraining himself, Mortimer noticed signs of a relentless economy everywhere. Pencils had been shaved down to the last half inch; cigarette butts went into a special jar, obviously to be broken and rolled once more.

"I still don't understand how you manage," Mortimer said.

"Come," Shalinsky said, leading him back into the kitchen. "People give me things." He chuckled, fingering some crumbs on the enamel-topped table. "I'm a character, Griffin. An embarrassment. You think I don't trade on it? So if I go to a rich Jew's office and he says to me no, I say, okay, *très bien*, no hard feelings, and I sit outside in his waiting room. Coughing. Bringing up phlegm. Can he throw me out, an old man? What would the goyim who come and go say? Me, I sit and wait. I read. I suck my teeth. Eventually if they don't give me money I get an old suit. If not that, something else. Paper and carbon from the office maybe . . ."

"Shalinsky, you're a blackmailer."

"What do they need paper for? Bookkeeping. But for a poet with a pencil and paper . . . *magic*, Griffin."

"All the same –"

"In some of these offices all they have to do is see me coming and right away the hand dips into the pocket to get rid of me. From people in the needle trade I get seconds, last year's numbers. Somewhere else I sell a subscription to *Jewish Thought*. Sure, they never read it. You think I don't know? What is it for them? A conversation piece. Something to keep on the coffee table. I care? Two quid is not to be sneezed at." Shalinsky squeezed his eyes together and groaned. "But my poor feet. Oi. The old gray mare, Griffin, she ain't what she used to be. Well, to what do I owe this honor? No. Don't tell me. You've brought me *quelque chose* for the magazine. A new essay. So, don't be shy. Your piece on Chagall, I don't mind telling you, was highly spoken of in influential quarters. I've heard many favorable comments."

"Why in the hell did you change the title?"

"Oh, that Daniels, he'll be the end of me. With him it always has to be snappy, up-to-the-minute. Could you pass me the kettle, please. The water's getting cold."

Grudgingly, Mortimer handed him the kettle.

"Ah, it's good." Shalinsky wiggled his toes. Under the nails the flesh was purple. "At my age, Griffin, once the sexual passions are spent, you'd be surprised what you enjoy." Shalinsky laughed, his cigarette clinging miraculously to his lips, ashes dribbling to his trousers and into the basin. "So you'd like some tea?"

Mortimer got up to look out of the window. His heart leaped. The car, a Vauxhall, that had started out after his taxi, was parked across the street.

"Add water to the kettle and –"

"I'm not sure I can stay much longer."

Shalinsky dried his feet, moaning pleasurably. "Griffin, you're an honest man . . ." He hesitated, his smile impish. "Well, about some things. Advise me. I have been thinking of publishing a slim volume of my *pensées* at my own expense. In the Continental tradition. But all my money seems to go on tinned foods and postage for parcels."

"What about your printing bills, Shalinsky?" Mortimer said drawing the curtains. "How do you manage that?"

"Oh, with Levitt I have a special deal. He's a unique chap." Shalinsky leaned closer to Mortimer. "You are looking into the face of a mortgaged man."

So are you, Mortimer thought.

"When I meet my Maker Levitt collects on the policy. He's my beneficiary. Well, some men will their bodies to science; me, I've sold mine for the arts. *C'est assez drôle, n'est-ce pas?* Well, Griffin, enough. Let us put down our swords. The truth will out. Why have you come to see me at such a late hour?"

"The truth is I came here to bash your teeth in."

"But," Shalinsky demanded eagerly.

"Well, the way you were sitting here . . . the parcels . . ."

"There! You see! Violence. Ach. *Pour les bêtes.* Among us, however –"

"God damn it, Shalinsky. I'm a wreck. I don't know whether I'm coming or going these days –"

"Have no fear, *chaver*. Society is sick, not you."

"The first time I spoke to you, you said I'd be famous one day. You were wrong, Shalinsky. I'm a ruined man."

Shalinsky sighed.

"My wife's thrown me over for another man. I've been tossed out of my own house."

Shalinsky nodded with ineffable sadness. "Mixed marriages," he said, "never work."

Mortimer pounded his fist against the table. "Why do I even sit here talking to you?"

"Ah, Griffin . . ."

"I've resigned my job at Oriole."

"Griffin, the scapegoat."

"There are killers seeking me out even now."

"Well, now you see, now you know. It's hard to be a Jew."

"I am not," Mortimer said, seizing Shalinsky by the shoulders and shaking him, "a Jew."

"But Griffin, Griffin, don't you see? A Jew is an idea. Today you're my idea of a Jew."

Mortimer leaped up to peer through the curtains. The Vauxhall was still there. He paced up and down the kitchen. "Shalinsky, one minute. Hold on there. The truth is I did bring you a manuscript."

"That explains it."

"*What?*"

"Why you're so nervous."

"Yes. Yes, of course." Mortimer placed the long brown envelope on the table. "Shalinsky, you are to guard this with your life. You are not to publish it until you hear from me."

The old man nodded.

"But, of course," Mortimer added, trying to appear casual, "if anything happens to me, you can publish immediately."

"What should happen to you?"

"A street accident. Anything. Who knows? But I must have this absolutely clear. If anything happens you publish immediately."

"Understood."

"Is that a promise, then?"

"Absolutely."

"Good," Mortimer said.

"You see, *chaver*. You can always rely on your own."

"I hope so. I certainly hope so. Good night, Shalinsky."

"*Au plaisir.*"

Artists, Shalinsky thought fondly, they're all the same. Children. Immediately, the front door had shut, he ripped open the long brown envelope. Naturally, it was about publishing, his world. Well, he had read better stories. Another Sholom Aleichem he certainly wasn't. For a fantasy, the language was too dry, even legalistic, and then of course the names would have to be changed. Shalinsky was willing to publish the story, he was loyal, but a libel suit, he thought, I can do without.

Thirty-Seven

MORTIMER RETURNED TO Polly's flat to wait. Nothing happened that night. Or the next day. Even more encouraging, there was no sign of the Vauxhall or the Rover. Is it possible, Mortimer thought, that I've scared him off? For the umpteenth time, he took out his Air Canada tickets and studied them. The suitcases were packed. Everything was ready. Finally, Polly came home late and weary from Oriole House. "Thank God you're here. Safe," he said.

Polly wrinkled her nose at him.

"I'll pour you a bath," he said.

"Lovely."

Mortimer turned on both taps, waited three minutes, and then joined her in the living room, where she had cut to, adorably pink and refreshed, in her dressing gown. What would I do without her, he thought adoringly.

"I feel like a new person," Polly said.

"I'll bet," he said warmly. "What kept you?"

"Oh, one of Dino Tomasso's emergency conferences. The Our Living History series is to be expanded."

"Is it, now?"

"It's to be *vastly* expanded to include, well, case histories, England Now, and all that jazz. Oh, darling, I'm so proud. I'm so happy for you."

"Why?"

"Because," she said. "Now hold on to your hat. Because, my darling, the first projected title in the England Now series is to be the biography of a professional man in his early forties –"

"*Mortimer Griffin's Story*," he said, shuddering.

"How ever did you guess?"

"Polly, do you trust me?"

"What a question! Why, I'd march over clifftops for you."

"Good. Because there's no time for explanations. In a nutshell, my dear, the Star Maker intends to have me murdered."

"Wow! So that's why you've been avoiding the office and drinking so much."

"Yes."

"I'm so relieved. I thought perhaps you were sorry . . . well, about us."

"Polly, will you come to Canada with me?"

"I'd go anywhere with you. Anywhere in the whole, wide world."

"We're leaving first thing in the morning. I've already made the reservations. He'll never find us in Canada, the obscene son-of-a-bitch."

A tear welled in Polly's eye.

"What's the matter?" he demanded.

"Of course I'll come with you . . ."

"But," he said wearily.

"Are you prepared to spend the rest of your life on the run, looking over your shoulder, waiting, knowing one night he'll be there?"

"What?"

"If the Star Maker is out to get you . . . well, shouldn't you stay here and make a fight of it?"

Mortimer went to pour himself a drink. An enormous drink.

"You won't find courage in there, darling."

"Our Father who art in heaven," he began, "hallowed be thy name . . ."

"I'm only saying this because I love you. I want you to be able to walk tall, Mortimer. Always."

Mortimer went to the window to peer through the curtains. The Vauxhall was there. So was the Rover. Herr Dr. Manheim got out, followed by his two assistants. They conferred with Dr. Laughton and Gail on the other side of the street.

"Christ," Mortimer said, grabbing for the phone. Nine nine nine; that would do the trick. "Polly," he said, his voice quivering, "the line's dead!"

"This is it, then," she said, enthralled.

Mortimer seized her. "Polly, listen to me. This is no movie. This is real. Understand?"

"Roger."

"Oh, my God."

"There isn't much time, is there? The sands are running out."

"Yes, yes. Now listen, I want you to slip out the back way and run – run, understand?"

"My place is here with you."

Mortimer beat himself on the forehead. He pulled his hair. "Listen to me, Polly," he said, shaking her. "We have one chance."

"Naturally," she said with appetite.

"I want you to run to the nearest phone booth and call the police. Nine nine nine. As soon as you've gone, I will open the curtains. Then I will set the table for two and pour myself a drink. I will talk. I will pretend you are in the kitchen. Now hurry, for Christ's sake. Hurry."

"It's a piece of cake," Polly said and, blowing him a kiss, she was gone.

Mortimer counted to ten and pulled the curtains. In full view of the parked cars, he poured two drinks and carried the glass of sherry into the kitchen, emerging again to set the table.

Polly ran. She ran and ran. The first telephone booth she came to was empty, which wouldn't have done at all. She continued, breathless, to the next booth where, fortunately, a long-haired teen-ager was chattering endlessly, unaware that a man's life was at stake. Rat-tat-tat, Polly went, banging her sixpence against the glass. Rat-tat-tat. The teen-ager was done, just in time, Polly sensed, and she entered the booth. Polly deposited her sixpence and dialed nine nine nine.

"Metropolitan Police here. Yes?"

Polly smiled warmly.

"Hello! Hello? Is there anyone there?" the officer asked.

Gratefully, Polly hung up, hung up without speaking, and on the wide screen that was her mind's eye, sirens sounded, police cars heaving into Beaufort Street in the nick of time. Crowds formed. They embraced. Somewhere in the night a bird was singing. Tomorrow the sun would come up. Tomorrow and tomorrow. Old Sol, she thought.

Afterword

BY MARGARET DRABBLE

Cocksure is a very cocksure novel. It launches itself at the literary and show business world of London in the Swinging Sixties as boldly as Mordecai Richler himself did when he came to take Europe by storm. Short, sharp, sexy, and witty, it is full of energy and invention. Reading it now is an odd experience. In part it's like stepping back into one's youth, into a time warp where the Beatles and Kenneth Tynan and Vidal Sassoon and all those cultural icons of the sixties were alive, well, and supremely confident: but it's also packed with warnings about the world which has come to be.

The London that I knew when I was in my twenties is instantly recognizable in these pages, and only just exaggerated – these were the days when primary school teachers were so conscientiously liberated that it's only just fantasy to imagine a group of children performing a piece by the Marquis de Sade as a school play, and being enjoined to use simple Anglo-Saxon language in the classroom. "The tigers of wrath are wiser than the horses of instruction" was the Blakean motto daubed on the walls of one particularly radical local school near my home in North London, and we were all enjoined not to nurse unsatisfied desires. The *Lady Chatterley* decision of 1960 had freed novelists from linguistic constraints, and theatre censorship by the antique office of the

Lord Chamberlain was lifted in 1968. Nudity came to the stage with *Hair* and *Oh! Calcutta!* (One of my college friends, Bernadine Wall, then an aspiring novelist and now a psychoanalyst, appeared for the defence in the Chatterley case, representing incorruptible student youth: she supported the radical argument that the book would be perfectly safe in the hands of girls, wives, and servants. I was to appear years later in 1977 for the defence in the *Gay News* blasphemy trial, representing the incorruptible literary housewife and mother-of-three. Her team won: we lost. They were allowed to produce evidence of literary merit: we weren't.)

In 1968 we hadn't yet achieved the freedom demanded by Richler's Ziggy Spicehandler who believed that "so long as you couldn't pull your cock on TV . . . artistic freedom was impaired," but it seemed well on the way. In 1965, as recorded in these pages, Kenneth Tynan had said "fuck" on television and wasn't prosecuted: everybody, including myself, was reading that classic and pseudonymous work of French pornography, *The Story of O*. Satire was the vogue, and the newly discovered concept of "the Establishment" was its target: Richler evokes the popular real-life program *TW3* (*That Was The Week That Was*) as well as inventing one of his own, wonderfully entitled *Insult*, in which old-fashioned heroes are subjected to merciless contemporary mockery for their outdated virtues.

The protagonist of this novel, Mortimer Griffin, a white Anglo-Saxon Protestant Canadian, is publicly insulted on this program for his wartime gallantry, and is simultaneously persecuted by a Jewish doppelgänger who prefigures the more fully realized and tragic shadow, Harry, who appears as persecutor in *St. Urbain's Horseman*. The appalling blackmailing Shalinsky insists that the circumcised Mortimer is really Jewish, throwing him into an agony of embarrassment and ideological conflict over his denial. Shalinsky sniffs ignoble anti-Semitism in everything Mortimer says, and Mortimer is bewildered in this world where any ethnicity other than his own is chic: his own conventional good looks are, he fears, suburban, and he suspects his cock is too small – but *how can he tell*? He feels left out of the world of Saul Bellow, and is understandably dismayed when his wife leaps into bed with his hairy friend Ziggy and gives up on deodorants.

Mortimer is in publishing, with the distinguished Oriole Press, but he is brought into violent contact with the world of Hollywood when the monstrous Star Maker from Hollywood arrives to buy up and take over. In the passages about the movie industry and its moguls, Richler takes up the theme of Aldous Huxley's Californian satire, *After Many a Summer* (1939), in which "Uncle Jo" Stoyte seeks eternal life, and like Tithonus discovers the shocking (yet perhaps, after all, acceptable?) price: there are echoes in both works of the dystopia of Laputa in Swift's *Gulliver's Travels*. In the Star Maker's dreams of androgynous reproduction (the inspiration for one of the best puns in this verbally inventive book) Richler accurately foresees a brave new world where the rich will be able to buy up the body parts of the poor. He is very funny about the bionically manufactured and tragically abused "Star," and mentions in passing a little heap of nude "used starlets lying on the living room rug" – a very sixties image, evoking all those movies full of starlets with long legs and beehive hairstyles and pouting Bardot lips. Richler creates a cinematic heroine, Polly, whose attractive existence is entirely dependent on the medium of the movie, who can cut and censor at will.

The sixties had their squalid side, and Richler here alludes to some of liberation's historical victims – politician John Profumo, caught out in a sex-and-spy scandal with Christine Keeler, and the persecuted homosexual Stephen Ward, who committed suicide in the wake of this disaster. In this climate director Peter Brook developed what Antonin Artaud had called "The Theatre of Cruelty," which reached its climax with his production of Peter Weiss's *Marat-Sade* in 1964 – I had forgotten until rereading this novel the experience of attending in some deeply uncomfortable venue a Peter Brook performance of a play about Christine Keeler's trial and imprisonment, which now, in retrospect, seems to have presaged so much of what happens on the Fringe. The sixties were to change the possibilities of what happens in film and television and theatre forever.

There were casualties and excesses and cruelties in Swinging London, which in itself, as Richler suggests, was perhaps in part a product of American magazine attention. But London existed with or without Hollywood and *Time* magazine, and the mood of the novel is full of a youthful and pristine zest. It recaptures much of the spontaneous innocence of those relatively unpackaged days when television plays were transmitted live from the studio to the nation. (My first husband, actor Clive Swift, says he was in Richler's first television play, and that they had to run from set to set to catch the camera.) Television series like *The Avengers*, devised by Richler's influential Canadian contemporary Sydney Newman, were considered kinky and kooky, but they had a most beguiling manner. They had both the simplicity and the tease of the mini-skirt.

Cocksure is a good-humoured book, which would be hard to write in today's climate, when we do not rely on the censor to hack at our work, but are encouraged to censor ourselves in the name of political correctness. It doesn't seem to worry about being sexist and racist, and it's full of risky jokes about Jews and blacks and queers and breasts and orgasms: it fights what Mortimer Griffin calls the tyranny of the minority. *St. Urbain's Horseman*, which was soon to follow, developed many of the themes, but in a more sombre vein. The topography of London, from Jewish Golders Green to seedy Soho, from the private wards of the London Clinic to the gay guardsmen-frequented pubs of Victoria, is accurate and lovingly observed, as are the oddities of British publishers – this was the point in time when publishing power was moving from the old respectable houses like Oriole, with their high-minded owners, to a wave of brasher, more commercial new-comers. *Plus ça change*, one might today remark.

This is a London I recognize. Some of its institutions have vanished – the Lyons Corner Houses have gone, and *TW3* and Peter Cook are dead. David Frost, one of the lesser stars of *TW3*, survives, and has been knighted by a grateful Tory government for interviewing its members so loyally and with so little satire for so many years. Prime Minister Harold Wilson, who in his time honoured the Beatles, and who presided over the explosion of energy that this book records, died after a long illness in May 1995: it's fashionable now to blame his government's progressive legislation (on abortion, divorce, homosexuality, censorship, education, racial discrimination) and his tolerance of the permissiveness of the sixties for crime and high unemployment today. I don't believe that makes sense.

This book is a firsthand witness, without hindsight, to what things were really like. Read it and decide. It's part of the evidence. Not all of sixties London, let alone of Britain, is reflected in this book, and I myself spent most of the decade not in celebrity hairdressing salons or television studios but pushing a double pushchair to the greengrocer's or to feed the ducks in the park. But what is here is real too. This is an absurd satirical fantasy, but at the same time it records how things were and hints at what they were about to become. For this brief moment, London was alive. It was a capital city. Life, like a television play, was improvised and under-rehearsed. Things were happening. Life was a happening. I don't know how dark Mordecai Richler intended his satire to be, but the effect of this novel is curiously exhilarating.

BY MORDECAI RICHLER

ESSAYS

Hunting Tigers Under Glass: Essays and Reports (1968)
Shovelling Trouble (1972)
Notes on an Endangered Species and Others (1974)
The Great Comic Book Heroes and Other Essays (1978)
Home Sweet Home: My Canadian Album (1984)
Broadsides: Reviews and Opinions (1990)

FICTION

The Acrobats (1954)
Son of a Smaller Hero (1955)
A Choice of Enemies (1957)
The Apprenticeship of Duddy Kravitz (1959)
The Incomparable Atuk (1963)
Cocksure (1968)
The Street (1969)
St. Urbain's Horseman (1971)
Joshua Then and Now (1980)
Solomon Gursky Was Here (1989)

FICTION FOR YOUNG ADULTS

Jacob Two-Two Meets the Hooded Fang (1975)
Jacob Two-Two and the Dinosaur (1987)
Jacob Two-Two's First Spy Case (1995)

HISTORY

Oh Canada! Oh Quebec!: Requiem for a Divided Country (1992)
This Year in Jerusalem (1994)

TRAVEL

Images of Spain (1977)